THE STORY OF LORD ROBERTS

THE STORY OF LORD ROBERTS

by

EDMUND F. SELLAR

LIVING BOOK PRESS

GET ALL OF THE 'HISTORY SHAPERS' BOOKS
The Story of...

David Livingstone	Robert Bruce	Chalmers of New
H. M. Stanley	General Gordon	Guinea
Abraham Lincoln	Lord Clive	Bishop Patteson
Sir Francis Drake	Captain Cook	Joan of Arc
Sir Walter Raleigh	Nelson	Napoleon
Columbus	Lord Roberts	Cromwell

PLEASE NOTE

In this series, you will read about historical figures who displayed courage, bravery, self-sacrifice, and many other admirable traits. Their stories remind us that many people in history took bold actions and made tough choices. Yet, even those who achieved great things sometimes held ideas or pursued goals that were not beneficial to everyone. History is full of complex individuals—parts of their lives inspire us to be brave and stand up for what is right, while other parts remind us to consider the unintended consequences of our actions.

As you explore these biographies, we invite you to reflect on the qualities that enabled these figures to achieve greatness and the lessons we can learn from their mistakes. Maybe you too can become a History Shaper—someone who learns from the past and helps to make our world a better place for everyone.

Contents

Early Days—Arrival in India

On the 30th September 1832, Frederick Sleigh Roberts was born at Cawnpore, in India.

Like so many of our great soldiers, Lord Roberts is an Irishman, and he is proud of the fact. His father, General Sir Abraham Roberts, was a distinguished soldier, and like his son spent the greater part of his life in India. While still a child of two years old, Sir Abraham and Lady Roberts brought their boy home to England.

Here they remained together for two years, after which the parents had to return to the East, and their child was left in the care of relatives at Clifton.

In common with so many children born in India, he was at first somewhat small and delicate.

His schooldays began early, as at the age of six he started doing lessons at a dame's school. In his eighth year he went to a school at Clifton kept by a Frenchman, Monsieur Desprez.

Here, though he was really eight years old, his small size and delicate appearance led him to be mistaken for a child of five.

This false idea of the boy's age and strength led to the downfall of one of his classmates. This latter was a

French boy about twice the size of Roberts, but a hulking, stupid fellow, who looked with jealousy on the little chap's cleverness and greater success at lessons. Unable to get above him in class, the Frenchman determined to take it out of his school-fellow by bullying.

One day a great outcry arose in the playground, and on a master hurrying up to see what the fuss was about, little Roberts was found lying on the ground, while the French bully was dancing about in a wild state of joy, and shouting out, "Me I have knock Freddy down! Me I have jump on him! Me I have dance on him!" All of a sudden his capers and song of victory ceased. Little Freddy recovered; quickly jumping to his feet, he landed his tormentor a good smack on the nose, straight from the shoulder, with his fist. The shouts of triumph changed to tears; the Frenchman was no boxer, and from that time he took care to leave the little English boy, who could use his fists in self-defence, severely alone.

At the age of ten young Roberts went to a preparatory school, and after remaining there for three years, he went to Eton, where he stayed a year, during which he gained a prize for mathematics; and this fact was recalled forty years later, when Etonians presented a sword of honour to their distinguished school-fellow on his return from victory in Afghanistan.

In January 1847 young Roberts, who had made up his mind to follow in his father's footsteps and become a soldier, entered Sandhurst.

Here he worked hard, and among other honours took a prize in German. His stay was not, however, to be a long one, as his father wished him to follow a career in India, rather than in the English army at home. So, after going to a military academy at Wimbledon, he at length secured a vacancy at the famous military college of the East India Company at Addiscombe.

Here the young man of eighteen began his military studies in real earnest, and he gave himself up to the study of "Fortification"; for already at this age he determined to get on in his profession, and we may be sure he was no idler.

His life at Addiscombe was a most happy one: he was popular with everybody, and had in especial five friends, who all chummed together, clubbing their pocket-money and having all things in common. Out of this common fund the fortunate member who got leave to spend a weekend in London was able to pay his expenses when his turn came.

Roberts rose to be corporal in the seminary, a position somewhat like a prefect at a public school, and we can well believe that his reign of authority was a mild and popular one, and that the junior cadets regarded him with the same feelings of affection as the soldiers in after years came to feel towards "Bobs," their popular and trusted Commander-in-Chief.

During his stay at Addiscombe, Roberts was by no

means strong. But as with Nelson, our greatest sailor, his good spirits and pluck more than made up for any delicacy.

His figure, though small and slight, was well-built. He was wiry and active, and always, we are told, very neat and careful about his dress.

At the end of the year 1851 Frederick Sleigh Roberts was gazetted a second lieutenant in the Bengal Artillery, and two months after the young cadet set sail for the land of his birth, where he was to become so famous. The departure of a cadet for India was in those days a much more serious affair than it is now. Leave could only be obtained—except in case of ill health—once, and that only after ten years in India, during an officer's whole service.

"Small wonder, then," Lord Roberts himself says, "that I felt as if I were bidding England farewell for ever when, on 20th February 1852, I set sail from Southampton with Calcutta for my destination."

The vast floating hotels which now cross the ocean were in those days undreamt of. Steamships were still in their infancy, the boats small and slow. The Suez Canal did not exist. People either had to go round the Cape to reach India, or else take the P. & O. to Alexandria; from thence the journey was made by river and canal to Cairo, from Cairo a diligence ran to Suez, and there the weary traveller had again to embark on a P. & O. which took him to Calcutta.

The steamer Roberts sailed in to Alexandria was the *Ripon*, commanded by Captain Moreby, a distinguished officer and a kind, fatherly man, especially attentive to the home-sick young "griffins"—as new arrivals in India are called.

The freshness and novelty of life at sea is a great cure for home-sickness. A passing ship, a school of porpoises, the sight of land—all become objects of excitement and interest. Then games of many and various kinds fill the time, and the passenger at his voyage's end usually steps on shore with a feeling of regret, and kindly feelings towards the trusty vessel which has reached port in safety, and which has, for the time being, been his home.

After Alexandria the journey across the desert was made in a vehicle like a bathing-machine, drawn by four mules, and in this Roberts and five other young cadets bumped and jolted from Cairo to Suez.

The sight of Cairo made a great impression on young Roberts. It was his first real view of the "gorgeous East," and he eagerly took in every detail of the sort of scenery which was to become in India so familiar to him.

At Suez the "griffins" embarked on the *Oriental*, and the terrific heat of that region was soon met with. Only those who have made the voyage know how great that heat may be. Should there be a following wind the stanchions and even the deck seem to be red-hot; and it is only by stopping and sailing full-speed astern that the ship can be cooled down and become a bearable habitation.

"I don't know how we shall fight in India if it is as hot as this," Roberts is said to have remarked.

At last, on the 1st of April, Calcutta was reached, and the young cadet stepped on shore in the land of his birth.

After a dreary dinner with an invalid officer of his own regiment (surely no cheerful omen!) young Roberts went to bed, regretting his many comrades of the ship, and feeling lonely and home-sick. Next morning at an early hour he was astir, and made the best of his way to Dum-Dum, where he lost no time in reporting himself and joining his regiment.

Here the same cheerless welcome waited him; there were scarcely any soldiers in the fort, and his second dinner in India, instead of consisting of a cheery mess-party, as he may have pictured, was a lonely meal with another subaltern.

The outlook was most depressing for a young man just arrived in the country.

"I became terribly home-sick, and convinced that I should never be happy in India," he afterwards used to relate.

One night, on the rare occasion of his dining out, he encountered on his way home a furious cyclone. His native servant was walking ahead of him with a lantern, but the light was soon blown out, and his guide continued on his way, thinking his master was following him. The latter shouted to his servant to stop, but the roar of the tempest drowned his cries. The night was pitch dark, several trees had been blown down, and huge branches were being driven through the air like thistle-down. Nearly blown off his feet, and in no little danger from the falling trees, it was only after weary hours wandering up and down and groping in the darkness that Roberts at length reached the safety of his own bungalow.

Next morning he sat down and wrote to his father, begging that if possible he might be sent to Burma. The old general replied with the glad news that he hoped shortly to be given the command of the large Peshawur division, when his son could then come and serve under him.

The young man hailed the news with delight; his dislike to India and his discontent vanished as if by magic; and when in August the wished-for order from his father came, he set forth with boyish eagerness for the frontier.

His journey thither took up nearly as much time as his whole stay at Dum-Dum. The macadamised road went no farther than Meerut; from there the remaining six hundred miles had to be made in a doolie or palanquin—a sort of sedan chair carried on men's shoulders. The heat was so great that travelling by day was impossible, and the stages had to be made by night. However, everything has an end, and at last, after being nearly three months on his journey, he reached Peshawur, where he found his father; and we can well imagine with what feelings of joy the pair greeted one another. They met "almost as strangers." "We did not, however," Lord Roberts himself tells us, "long remain so. His affectionate greeting soon put an end to any feeling of shyness on my part, and the genial and kindly spirit which enabled him to enter into and to sympathise with the feelings and aspirations of men younger than himself rendered the year I spent with him at Peshawur one of the brightest and happiest of my early life."

At Peshawur—Meeting with Nicholson

During his journey up to Peshawur Roberts had rested at Cawnpore, which was his birthplace. At Meerut he saw for the first time a body of the famous Bengal Horse Artillery, a force which has been described as "unsurpassed and unsurpassable." All the young soldier's ambition was fired to become one day a member of this grand corps, and he had already formed "a fixed resolve to leave no stone unturned in the endeavour to become a horse-gunner."

In the meanwhile, however, Roberts lived with his father, and had a tremendous amount of work to do. His duties were twofold, for he not only acted as his father's aide-de-camp, but also continued to do his duty as officer with the 2nd Company 2nd Battalion of the Bengal Artillery (known locally as "The Devil's Own ").

On the 1st of January 1853, Lord Roberts relates that he was at a dinner-party when the unlucky number thirteen sat down. It would be in accordance with the superstition could we relate the after-fate of the party by death and misadventure. Strange to say, the very opposite has to be chronicled. No less than eleven years after all the thirteen were alive, having passed through the terrible times of the Mutiny, during which five or six had been wounded.

In the autumn of the same year the health of old General Roberts began to fail, and he was, under advice from the doctors, obliged to leave India for good. So weak and ill was he that his son thought it his duty to accompany him part of the way down to Calcutta.

While travelling with his father Roberts missed his first chance of seeing active service and "smelling powder." There was trouble on the frontier; a number of the Bari villages were in revolt, and an expedition had to be sent to punish them. Although the young lieutenant galloped back as fast as relays of ponies could carry him, it was no good. He heard, indeed, the guns of "The Devil's Own " booming in the distance, but by the time he came up, to his grief and disappointment he found the fighting was over, and his baptism of fire was not yet to take place.

He was, however, to encounter another enemy of the British soldier in India, and during the winter he became very ill with fever. So serious was his illness that he was granted six months' leave of absence. This time he spent in a most delightful trip to Kashmir, on which he was accompanied by another lieutenant of artillery. The two young men had a splendid holiday; the country is one of the most beautiful and fertile in the world. The climate is good, and especially refreshing are the cool nights and fine early mornings, after the continual heat of the plains.

Thoroughly set up by the change, our hero returned

to Peshawur, and here he reached the height of his boyish ambition in receiving shortly afterwards the coveted "jacket" of a lieutenant in the Bengal Horse Artillery—the force he had set his heart on joining.

They were, indeed, a splendid body of men, mostly Irishmen, and great, strapping fellows, "almost all big enough to have lifted him from the ground with one hand." In such a crack corps good horsemanship was a point of honour with all, and Roberts soon set himself to become a good rider. So successful was he that he was chosen to ride in the regimental brake, which was drawn by six horses, ridden postillion fashion by three officers.

Again the old enemy, fever, laid him low, and once more the doctors sent him to Kashmir to get better. From Kashmir he set out on a four hundred miles' march to the famous hill station, Simla, and here came the "turning-point" in his career.

He was asked to lunch one day with Colonel Becher, the Quartermaster-General. After some talk, Colonel Becher, struck by the young man's soldierly qualities, told him he wished he could have him attached to his department. An appointment of this sort was sure to bring with it a rapid rise in his profession, and Lieutenant Roberts jumped at the idea. From that time it was the goal before him, till in the spring of 1856, far sooner than he had dreamt of, the Deputy-Assistant-Quartermaster-General was required for special service, and Roberts was offered the post.

His delight, however, soon received a check; his

appointment could not be sanctioned because he had not passed the necessary examination in Hindustani. This was to be held shortly. Nothing daunted, the young lieutenant engaged a native teacher, and set to work with all his might to learn the language. The time was short, but he made the most of it, and when July and the examination came, he passed the test with flying colours.

Shortly after he got what he had wished for: the vacancy was given him, and he was now a staff-officer, with every prospect of speedy success.

While on tour in his new capacity he received an offer which, had he accepted it, would have changed his whole life, and one of her greatest soldiers would have been lost to the country. This was none other than the chance of a post in the Public Works Department. The salary would, of course, have been far larger than that of an officer in the army, but Roberts was a soldier and the son of a soldier, and he determined to stick to his profession, so the offer was gratefully declined.

In order to join General Reed on a tour of inspection, Roberts accomplished a wonderful ride of a hundred miles in eleven hours, with but one short rest for refreshment. During this tour of inspection Roberts met for the first time a young subaltern in the Inniskilling Fusiliers, who will always be associated with the heroic exploits of the British army, and who many years after, as Sir George White, engraved his name on the annals of our race by the heroic manner in which he "kept the flag flying" at Ladysmith during the dark days of the Boer War.

An incident worth telling, as showing how unprepared everybody was for the outbreak of the Great Mutiny, came under the young staff-officer's notice at Nowshera.

The 55th Native Infantry were stationed there, and their colonel, who had been hitherto used to clean-shaven Hindu Sepoys, was loud in his complaints of the big-bearded Sikhs who had lately been enlisted in his regiment, and who he declared quite spoilt the smart, trim appearance of the ranks on parade.

Two months later the Hindus had broken out into mutiny: of all the regiment only the despised Sikhs remained loyal, and the colonel, who had declared he would stake his life on his trusty Hindustanis, mad with grief and disappointment, blew out his brains.

While in these parts Roberts met for the first time that modern hero of romance, the great John Nicholson. Perhaps no man ever impressed him more, either before or since, and Nicholson was a fit hero for a young soldier's worship and respect.

Like Roberts, he came of Irish stock, though his ancestors had, in the reign of Elizabeth, been sturdy Cumberland dalesmen who had emigrated to Ireland. He had come out to India as a boy of sixteen, and nearly all his time had been spent keeping order among the unruly tribes of the frontier.

The natives literally worshipped him as a god: he had

been known to flog the men who knelt before him in prayer as to a god-like saint. The tribesmen looked on him as no mere mortal man. "You could hear the ring of his horse's hoofs from Attock to the Khyber," ran the saying on the frontier.

John Nicholson was a man of splendid size and strength, six foot two in height, and of commanding aspect. "He was a man cast in a giant mould, with massive chest and powerful limbs, and an expression ardent and commanding, with a dash of roughness: features of stern beauty, a long black beard, and a sonorous voice. His imperial air never left him." No wonder this modern crusader fired the imagination of the keen young soldier.

"Nicholson," says Lord Roberts, "impressed me more profoundly than any man I had ever met before, or have ever met since. I have never seen any one like him. He was the beau-ideal of a soldier and a gentleman...." The great man soon showed a regard and affection for the ardent young officer, and the two were together almost from that hour until Nicholson's heroic death in the streets of Delhi.

The Mutiny

On his return to Peshawur Roberts had looked forward to hard work and a long spell of routine, but the outbreak of the great Indian Mutiny was to provide him with a more exciting field of activity.

The year 1857 broke with the threatenings of coming trouble. The Sepoys were restless, and seemed to obey their orders sulkily. During the months of February, March, and April, mysterious "chupatties," or cakes, were sent about the country, passed from hand to hand, and this was thought to be a means of telling the natives to rise, and a secret signal for them to get ready.

We must remember that, for the first few years of British rule in India, Hindus and Mohammedans had been happy to dwell peacefully side by side. They were thankful for the change from bloodshed and strife to law and order, under just rulers. They could no longer be tortured and robbed by their native kings, for the country was quiet and prosperous, and the poor man could live and labour without fearing the tyranny of the rich.

By-and-by, however, the people began to forget how poor and ill-treated they had been in the past. The Mohammedans looked back with regret on their days of power and splendour, when they had ruled India; while the Hindus thought of how they had got rid of the Mohammedan yoke.

Neither people liked to be ruled and to be under the power of a strange white people, who had come from across "the great water," and conquered their country with a mere handful of men. At this stage, the enemies of our rule spread a report that the English had made up their minds to destroy the religions of the two great races in India, and force them all to become Christians.

To a Hindu a cow is a sacred animal; on the other hand, the pig the Mohammedan holds in abomination, and he will sooner starve than even touch the flesh of what to him is an unclean beast. A report arose, and was busily spread about the country, that the new cartridges issued to the Sepoys, or native soldiers, had been greased with a mixture of cows' fat and lard. To touch one of these cartridges was to a native of either race a sin, and a great and unpardonable sin, against his religion. As explaining this feeling, Lord Roberts tells a story of a Sepoy, on his way to cook his food, with his "Iota," or tin drinking-vessel, full of water. He was met by a low-caste man employed in the Enfield Cartridge Factory, who begged him for a drink from his Iota. This Sepoy, a Brahmin—one of the highest caste—refused, saying, "I have scoured my Iota; you will defile it by your touch."

"Oh," sneered the low-caste native, "you think much of your caste, but wait a little; the Sahib-log "(that is,

European officers) "will make you bite cartridges soaked in cows' fat, and then where will your caste be?"

The Sepoy, no doubt, believed the man, and told his comrades what was going to happen. No wonder, then, that the soldiers believed the reports, and feared that by means of the new cartridges they were to be forced to change their religion.

At the time we speak of the British force in India numbered only 36,000 men, while there were some 257,000 native soldiers. The old belief that the British soldier was invincible, a belief which arose from the way in which mere handfuls of our men had broken and beaten large armies, met with a rude shock during the Afghan War, 1841—42. What the Afghans had shown to be possible the Sepoys might also accomplish. At all events, they had made up their minds to try.

Over the whole land there blew "a devil's wind," as the Hindus called it. The aged King of Delhi, when asked afterwards to explain the cause of the outbreak, answered, "I do not know. I suppose my people gave themselves up to the devil."

A mysterious prophecy was revived, and was repeated all over the country, from mouth to mouth.

In 1757, the Battle of Massy, Clive's victory which gave us India, had been fought and won. The English "raj," or rule, would run exactly one hundred years—so ran the prophecy; and lo! here was 1857—the hundred years had run their course.

The British forces were scattered in small detachments over Bengal, and most of the artillery was in native hands. Indeed, perhaps among the various causes of the Mutiny, it was the natives' sense of power—they had fought our battles and conquered for us, they argued—which urged them to rebel.

On the 11th of May, while Roberts and the other officers were sitting at mess in Peshawur, the bolt fell from the blue. In breathless haste a telegraphic signaler rushed in, and gasped out the startling news that an outbreak had occurred at Meerut, that Delhi had joined the rebels, and that many residents and officers at both stations had been murdered.

To fully understand the situation we must leave Lord Roberts for a little, and go back to relate the events which gave rise to the outbreak of the Mutiny, during which the whole power of British rule seemed at one moment to be tottering on its throne: a power which was only afterwards to be more firmly established, thanks to the heroic devotion and bravery of our men and their dusky allies who remained steadfast and true to their salt, while their comrades-in-arms on all sides rose in revolt.

As early as the 6th of February, an officer of the 34th Native Regiment had been warned by a Sepoy that his men, fearing that they were going to be forced to become Christians, meant to rise in revolt. We have already told the story of the Brahmin and the low-caste man at Dum-Dum.

The air was full of warnings had the authorities but

been alive to the fact. Already General Hearsay had written to the Government, "We are on a mine ready for explosion," and his words and warning were but too true. At Barrackpore, March 29th, on a Sunday afternoon, the match that was to explode the whole mine may be said to have been lighted.

The 34th were drawn up on parade, or rather the quarter-guard of the regiment—tall, fine, soldierly men—were drawn up in regular order. The rest of the regiment were in a wild state of excitement and disorder, chattering and gesticulating as only natives can.

In front of them a drug-maddened, excited Sepoy, named Mungal Pandy, stalked up and down. He shouted to his comrades to leave their ranks.

"Through biting these cartridges we shall all be made infidels! Be true to your faith, if you are not dogs! Show yourselves men; come out, and let the cursed Sahibs see that we are not afraid!"

Thus he marched to and fro, taunting the men with their cowardice; they were giving up their religion; they were accursed in this world, and with no hope of being saved in the next.

His words acted like magic, and struck home to his eager listeners; murmurs were heard, and the ranks swayed backwards and forwards. At this moment Lieutenant Baugh, the adjutant, roused from his afternoon's sleep by the news of a revolt, galloped upon the scene. Straight at Mungal Pandy he rode; there was a flash from the Sepoy's musket, and the horse went down. The gallant Englishman gets up, bruised and half-stunned as he is, and dashes in at the rebel. He misses his aim, and the first victim of the Indian Mutiny falls under Mungal Pandy's sword.

Hardly had Baugh fallen than the English serjeant-major ran up, hastily buttoning his tunic, hot and blown with his dash across the parade-ground. All breathless as he was, he launches himself straight at the Sepoy's face: the latter is a skilled swordsman, and the brave Englishman, taken at a disadvantage, is cut down. Two of the Sahibs are killed, no startling retribution has followed, and the hitherto loyal quarter-guard refuse to seize the mutineer, though they run forward to do so in a half-hearted manner.

Just then General Hearsay rides up, to quote Mr. Fitchett, "a red-faced, wrathful, hard-fighting, iron-nerved veteran, with two sons, of blood as warlike as their father's, riding behind him as aides."

"Have a care, his musket is loaded!" somebody sang out.

"D—n his loaded musket! If I fall, John, rush in and put him to death somehow," shouted the general to his son.

The native officer, with Hearsay's pistol at his head, fell in with his men, and advanced to seize the mutineer, but Mungal Pandy has done his work. His excitement has left him, the knowledge of his crime remains. He is a brave man, however, though a rebel, and will take his fate in his own hands. Putting the muzzle of his rifle to his own body, he pulls the trigger with his naked toe and falls shot through the breast.

Discipline had for the moment again asserted itself, and the absolute fearlessness of Hearsay had for the time being won the day.

Not long after, at Meerut, the flames of mutiny thus promptly quenched broke out in earnest. Towards the end of April a feeling of restlessness and discontent began to show itself: the Sepoys became less respectful towards their officers, and almost insolent in their bearing. Fires also broke out in the lines at night, and some troopers of the 3rd Light Cavalry actually refused to take the new cartridges. Eighty-five men of the 3rd were tried, accordingly, by a court-martial consisting of six Mohammedan and nine Hindu officers. They were found guilty, and sentenced to ten years' imprisonment with hard labour.

On the 9th of May there was a parade of the whole Meerut garrison: before their comrades the eighty-five troopers were brought forth, sentence read, and the fetters slowly and laboriously fastened on them. Each man in turn called for his comrades to rescue him, but as yet each man called in vain. Under the pitiless scorching sun the work of degradation went on; occupying as it did several hours, the ceremony ceased to impress, and inspired anger rather than fear in the hearts of the Sepoys.

The next day was a Sunday. Outwardly, things seemed peaceful and calm; the lesson read to the mutineers, it was hoped, had taken effect, but in the bazaars and elsewhere there was a spirit of unrest. Still the British officers were confident in the loyalty of their men, and their suspicions, which ought to have been awakened, were strangely lulled into a feeling of false security.

The chaplain of Meerut was about to start for church accompanied by his wife, when their faithful native nurse fell on her knees before them and begged them to stay at home. "There was going to be a fight with the Sepoys," she kept on saying. The clergyman pooh-poohed her fears, but his wife believed the woman, and at her request he took his children with him instead of leaving them alone with their ayah.

He soon saw that the native woman had spoken the truth. Before the church was reached the rattle of musketry was heard. On arrival at the door the buglers of the both were sounding the "alarm" and the "assembly"; the parade was hastily dismissed, and the British soldiers rushed to the barracks for their arms and ammunition.

Fortune to a certain extent favoured our men. The mutineers had expected to find the both in church, unarmed save for their bayonets. By a lucky chance, however, church on this particular Sunday had been put off for half-an-hour, and as the rebels galloped down the lines of the both they found the men fully armed and in the act of falling in.

Without a moment's delay the 3rd Native Cavalry dashed to the gaol, broke into the cells, set free their eighty-five comrades, and all other prisoners as well. While this was going on the two Native Infantry regiments, in a wild state of excitement, set fire to their tents, and began firing their muskets at random.

In vain the British officers tried to restore order. The Sepoys would not actually attack their own officers, but telling them that the Company's raj was over, begged them to get away while they could in safety; officers of other regiments they did not spare, and showed no feelings about shooting them down. While exhorting his own men of the 11th to remain true to their salt, Colonel Finnis, who had served with Sepoys for forty years, and fully trusted in their loyalty, fell riddled with bullets from the muskets of the loth.

The fall of Colonel Finnis was the signal for a general rising. Seven officers, the wives of three officers, two children, and every stray European found—man, woman, and child—were ruthlessly massacred. The work of murder went on apace; the streets were in a blaze; by the light from the flames the Sahibs were discovered; every hated white man was chased and cut to pieces.

"When day broke Meerut showed streets of ruins, blackened with fire and splashed red with the blood of murdered Englishmen and Englishwomen."

And now the die had been cast: the Sepoys had betrayed their salt; they were murderers and traitors, and could look for no mercy if caught. In Delhi, they learnt from the native officers of the court-martial sent to try them, the troops were all ready to join them and revive the old Mogul rule.

"To Delhi! To Delhi!" was their cry, as the murderers galloped off, leaving behind them nothing but smouldering fires and the dead and mutilated bodies of their officers and victims.

Amid this tale of treachery and crime there is one bright incident of native loyalty worth telling. A Hindu native officer had warned Lieutenant Gough, of the 9th Light Cavalry, that there was going to be serious trouble. Gough had repeated the tale to his colonel, and also to the brigadier, General Wilson, but both had thought lightly of the news.

The following day, that fateful Sunday, the same native officer, attended by two troopers, galloped to Gough's house, shouting that the "hala" had begun, and that the Native Infantry were firing on their officers. Saddling his horse, the Englishman set off at full gallop for the parade ground, attended by the three natives. The Sepoys called to the troopers to get out of the way, as they meant to shoot the Sahib. No notice being taken of this, they fired, but missed the whole party.

The lieutenant with his trusty escort then turned and galloped to the lines of the 9th Cavalry. Here the men were saddling up and helping themselves to ammunition. A recruit or two fired at him, but the old soldiers were loyal; and the native officers flocked round him and implored him to go away, telling him that they could not answer for his safety.

Darkness was coming on as Gough rode towards the European lines and charged through the crowded bazaars. In sight of the Artillery mess the faithful natives left him. They had seen their Sahib safe, had protected him at the risk of their lives, but they could not leave their relations and friends, with whom they had determined to throw in their lot. With a respectful "salaam" they bade farewell to the officer whose life they had saved, and galloped off to join their rebel comrades, nor could any trace of them afterwards be found.

General Hewitt has been much blamed for not starting in pursuit of the mutineers on their way to Delhi. The officers of the Carabineers begged hard to be allowed to avenge their fallen comrades. The Rifles, 1000 strong, were ready and eager for the fray. Lord Roberts himself, however, considers that pursuit would have been useless.

"The Carabineers," he says, "were but lately arrived from England, and were composed largely of recruits still in the riding-school, while their horses were, for the most part, quite unbroken. *No action, however prompt, on the part of the Meerut authorities could have arrested the Mutiny.* The Sepoys," he continues, "had determined to throw off their allegiance to the British Government, and the 'when' and the 'how' were merely questions of time and opportunity."

The Mutiny (Continued)

"Fortunately for India there were good men and true" (to use Lord Roberts' own words) "at Peshawur in those days, when hesitation and irresolution would have been fatal."

Immediately on hearing the news, the Commissioner Edwardes, acting with his deputy, Nicholson, sent to the post-office and seized all native letters. These on being opened and read showed that the worst fears were only too well grounded. Every native regiment in the garrison was in the plot, and prepared at the earliest opportunity to join the rebels.

Two days after the news came to Peshawur, Roberts was ordered to attend a meeting at the general's house. The problem to be solved was how the Punjab could best be made secure with the small force of British troops available—all told, not more than 15,000, with 84 guns, against upwards of 65,000 natives, with 62 guns.

It was decided that the only chance of keeping the Punjab quiet was to trust the chiefs and the people, and to try and get them to ride with us against the Hindustanis. Nor was this confidence misplaced; the chiefs along the border proving again, as they had already done in the Sikh War, how loyal and trustworthy they were.

It was also arranged that a movable column, made up of reliable troops, should be formed in the Punjab, and be kept ready to move and strike whenever its services might be required. Brigadier Neville Chamberlain was appointed to the command of the column, and Lieutenant Roberts, to his great delight, was chosen as one of the staff.

The night of the conference might have been Roberts' last. The guard which kept watch outside his bungalow was furnished by the 64th Native Infantry, a regiment with a bad reputation. The letters, which had been taken from the post-office and opened, showed it to be on the verge of mutiny, and it was to be ordered to leave Peshawur the following morning.

"I could not help feeling," says Lord Roberts, "as I lay down on my bed, which, as usual in the hot weather, was placed in the verandah for coolness, how completely I was at the mercy of the sentry who walked up and down within a few feet of me. Fortunately he was not aware that his regiment was suspected, and could not know the reason for the sudden order to march, or my career might have been ended then and there."

Within a week from that time Roberts started for Rawal Pindi to be ready to join the movable column, which was to be formed as soon as the troops could be got together.

"I took with me," he tells us, "only just enough kit for a hot-weather march, and left everything standing in my house just as it was, little thinking that I should never return to it or be quartered in Peshawur again."

With General Neville Chamberlain, Roberts left Peshawur and went to Rawal Pindi, where he was for some time employed doing confidential work in the office of Sir John Lawrence, the Chief Commissioner. Sir John was all for the policy of striking while the iron was hot. Delhi was in the hands of the mutineers, and must at all costs be retaken. To the Commander-in-Chief, General the Hon. George Anson (who, as an ensign, was present at Waterloo), he wrote, imploring him to press on to the city's recapture.

"When have we failed when we acted vigorously?" he asked. "When have we succeeded when guided by timid counsels? Clive, with 1200 men, fought at Plassy in opposition to the advice of his leading officers; beat 40,000 men and conquered Bengal."

One of the native princes, the Maharajah of Patiala, whom Lawrence was all along for trusting at this juncture, came to our aid and proved his loyalty.

"Maharajah Sahib," he was asked, "answer me one question: Are you for us or against us?"

"As long as I live, I am yours," was the answer. "What do you want done?"

Patiala was true to his word, and throughout the Mutiny the Phulkan chiefs stood firm and did us trusty service.

While Lieutenant Roberts was still at Rawal Pindi it became known that the mutineers were going to make their great stand at Delhi, and the order came that the troops from the Punjab were to be sent thither. On the 2nd of June the movable column entered Lahore, to the great joy of the Europeans in the city, who had been anxiously awaiting its arrival.

At Lahore Roberts first saw the grim realities of the stirring times in which he was living. He was sharing a bungalow with the brigadier, when, during the night, a spy awoke him and said that the 35th Native Regiment, which was attached to the column, intended to revolt, and that some of the men had already got their muskets loaded.

Roberts at once awoke General Chamberlain and told him the report. Next morning a drumhead court-martial, composed of native officers, was ordered to try the case. Two Sepoys, whose muskets were found to be loaded, were found guilty of mutiny and sentenced to death. The carrying out of this sentence made a great impression on the young officer. To quote his own words:

"Chamberlain decided that they should be blown away from guns in the presence of their own comrades, as being the most awe-inspiring means of carrying it into effect. It was a terrible sight," he continues, "and one likely to haunt the beholder for many a long day; but that was what was intended."

The condemned men went to their doom calmly and showed no fear: their comrades were taken aback at the swift and terrible punishment, but it in no way altered their resolve to desert to Delhi on the earliest chance they might have to do so.

Two days after this the column left and came to Jullundur, and, General Chamberlain having left for Delhi, Roberts' hero, John Nicholson, took over the command. Jullundur was garrisoned by the troops of the Rajah of Kapurthala. These evidently thought that the British rule in India was at an end, and were in consequence most swaggering and insolent.

A *durbar*, or council, was arranged, at which Roberts was present, and was an eye-witness of the scene between the Rajah's general, Mehtab Sing, and Nicholson. After the durbar was over, Mehtab Sing was walking to the door, when the stalwart form of Nicholson appeared in front of him, barring the native general's further progress.

"Do you see that General Mehtab Sing has his shoes on?" he sternly asked. "If I were the last Englishman left in Jullundur you should not come into my room with your shoes on." Then, politely turning to Commissioner Lake, "I hope the Commissioner will allow me to order you to take your shoes off and carry them out in your own hands, so that your followers may witness your discomfiture."

For a native to enter the presence of an Englishman with his shoes on is, to his mind, the greatest insult he can offer a white man. Never before the Mutiny would the Kapurthala general have dared to act in such a way. Now, completely cowed, Mehtab Sing did meekly as he was bidden, and walked to the door, his shoes in his hand.

Six years later Roberts was on a pig-sticking expedition with the Rajah of Kapurthala, who, when he heard that his guest had been at the Commissioner's house during the scene we have told, laughed heartily and said, "Oh, then you saw Mehtab Sing made to walk out of the room with his shoes in his hands? We often chaff him about that little affair, and tell him that he richly deserved the treatment he received from the great 'Nicholson Sahib.'"

On the column reaching Philour, it was determined to disband the 35th Native Infantry. The native troops had as yet caused no trouble, but it was feared that when Delhi was reached they would try to desert. Quickly and silently the British troops took up their position; the two batteries in the centre, the guns unlimbered and ready for action.

Roberts himself was told off to give the commanding officer orders to disarm and dismiss his regiment. Surrounded by our own troops the native soldiers were ordered to pile arms and take off their belts.

Both officers and Sepoys were equally taken aback; the former had no idea of what was going to happen, while the latter had hoped they would be able to slip off to Delhi with their arms. Major Younghusband, the commanding officer, had been with the 35th for thirty-three years. He was proud of his regiment, with which he had served in the Afghan War, where they had fought with great bravery, but now even he felt his men could not be trusted; and when he heard the order he could only murmur "Thank God!"

After the 35th had been disbanded, the 33rd arrived. The loyalty of this regiment was like-wise doubtful, and it was decided that the men should be dealt with in like manner. The British officers of the 33rd did not, however, take things so quietly. Their colonel trusted them to the death. On hearing what was to take place, he exclaimed, "What! disarm my regiment! I will answer with my life for the loyalty of every man."

"On my repeating the order," Lord Roberts relates, "the poor old fellow burst into tears."

"You have drawn the fangs of one thousand snakes— truly your luck is good!" was the remark of an old Sikh colonel who saw the ceremony.

Meanwhile an order had come from the Commander-in-Chief, asking that all artillery officers who could be spared should be sent to Delhi. Next morning the young lieutenant set off in high spirits. From Philour he went to Ludhiana. Here there was a block: all the vehicles were in use, and a long delay seemed in store for him when he, by good fortune, managed to get a seat on an extra mail-cart laden with ammunition, on the condition that his kit must be of the smallest, as there was no room for anything inside the cart.

Greatly pleased at his luck, Roberts describes himself "as like a boy at school who has got a hamper from home." He determined to share his success, and managed to squeeze, with two other officers to whom he had offered a lift, into the cart.

Near Delhi their driver pulled up, and refused to go any farther: the enemy were constantly on the road, threatening the rear of our troops, and the cart and its occupants might at any time drive into the middle of them. The officers let the driver get out and drove on themselves, hearing more plainly the booming of the guns, and passing by the wayside many dead bodies and other signs of warfare.

As they neared the city they came to a place where the road divides—one branch going through the cantonment, the other leading straight to the town. Fortunately for them-selves they chose the right road—to have followed the other would have landed them right in the middle of the foe—and pushed on through the growing darkness as fast as their tired ponies would go. At last they reached the British lines and safety.

"The relief to us when we found ourselves inside our own piquets may be imagined," says Lord Roberts.

On arrival his father's old staff officer, Henry Norman, who was then Assistant-Adjutant-General at headquarters, welcomed him most warmly, and very kindly asked the young artillery officer to share his tent. Dead-beat, Roberts was very soon sleeping the sleep of the weary. Next morning he awoke quite refreshed, none the worse for his long and dangerous journey, and above all, overjoyed to find himself at Delhi, and that the fighting was still going on.

The Ridge at Delhi

Delhi, the city of the Great Mogul, may be said to have been the centre and heart of the Mutiny. Hither, as we have seen, the mutineers fled after the outbreak at Meerut on May 11. The native regiments in the town joined them, and a general massacre of Europeans followed. To Delhi flocked all the rebels, and soon the city was filled with fierce, warlike troops, who knew that there was now no turning back or hope of mercy, and that they were fighting with their backs to the wall. The Delhi Field Force, which was sent to retake the stronghold, at first numbered only 3000 men, and afterwards it never rose above 9000 fighting men.

From the outset the force showed its splendid fighting qualities and power of hard-hitting. As far back as the 30th of May, 700 British soldiers beat and routed seven times their number of Sepoys, capturing five guns and a large quantity of stores and ammunition. Next day the enemy again attacked, and again our men drove them back in head-long confusion. The natives were learning the lesson that the British rule would continue as long as there were Britons left to shoulder a musket.

To quote Lord Roberts: "The Sepoys were no match for

British bayonets; and they now learnt that their misdeeds were not to be allowed to go unpunished." On the arrival of Roberts, the British Army, in which we include the loyal native troops, was posted on a ridge about sixty feet high, and varying in distance from the city from 1200 yards on the right, to 4 miles at the end near the river Jumna.

The Flagstaff Tower, which became the rendezvous for all non-combatants, was about one mile and a half away. It was here that the residents of Delhi assembled to make a stand on hearing of the outbreak at Meerut. The heat was almost unbearable to the closely packed throng of men, women, and children. No help seemed to be coming as they anxiously scanned the horizon towards Meerut, and at last, before dark, it was decided to leave and take the road to Umballa. They were only just in time; for before the last of the party were out of sight the natives poured in. Had they found the Sahibs there, all must have been killed.

Among the fugitives were Captain Tytler and his wife, who, after some hair-breadth escapes, arrived in safety at Umballa. This couple afterwards joined the camp at Delhi, where, on the 21st of June, Mrs. Tytler gave birth to a baby. This infant was christened "Stanley Delhi Force Tytler," and a soldier was heard to say: "Now we shall get our reinforcements. This camp was formed to avenge the blood of innocents, and the first reinforcement sent to us is a new-born infant." Sure enough, fresh troops did join the camp the very next day.

For the first two months General Barnard and the British force were fully occupied in defending themselves on the Ridge. The time for attacking the city had not yet come, and the little army had to fight for its very existence. The morning after General Barnard occupied the Ridge, the famous Corps of the Guides arrived in camp, "as fresh as if they had returned from an ordinary field-day, instead of having come off a march of nearly 600 miles, accomplished in the incredibly short time of twenty-two days, at the most trying season of the year. That very afternoon they showed their worth by driving the enemy back to Delhi, after a fierce hand-to-hand fight. Close up to the walls, Quintin Battye, the daring commander of the Guides Cavalry, got his death-wound. He might have had a great career; the Guides adored him, and would have followed him anywhere. Seldom, we are told, had a young soldier given such early promise of a brilliant future. Always fond of quotations, his last words were: *Dulce et decorum est pro patria mori* (" A sweet and comely thing it is to die for one's country ").

The Guides had found in camp a soldier after their own heart, who had been their leader in many a gallant charge. This was Hodson, of Hodson's Horse—"a tall, fair-haired man, with bloodless complexion; heavy, curved moustache; keen, alert, and, what some one called, 'unforgiving eyes.'" As the Guides rode in Hodson met them, and was greeted with wild cries of welcome.

"They seized my bridle," he says, "my dress, hands,

and feet, and threw themselves down before the horse with tears streaming down their faces."

Five days before Roberts arrived came the centenary of Plassy, and the Sepoys, by a more than usually fierce attack, determined to fulfil the prophecy that the British rule should only run a hundred years. For eight hours the attack continued; every man in the camp was engaged, and both sides fought with desperate fury. The Sepoys were "thousands against a mere handful," but they could do nothing against the steady valour of our men, and at last they were put to flight with the loss of over 1000 men. So the anniversary of Plassy came and went, and the British rule was still undefeated. The heat had been terrific: a hot wind was blowing, and there was a pitiless glare. After the battle men lay down where they had fought, quite done up; even the Ghurkas were worn out.

On the 30th of June, Roberts, who had taken up his duties as D.A.Q.M.G. to the Artillery, was under fire for the first time.

The next day the first regimental band to reach the camp arrived, playing the lively strains of "Cheer, Boys, Cheer!"

The fighting continued daily, with equal fury on both sides. Our loyal allies, the Ghurkas, were doing splendid service. The first time the mutineers encountered them they halted, said that they were brothers and should not kill one another, and begged them to come out and help to destroy the Sahibs. The Ghurkas listened in silence — the

Sepoys thought they had persuaded them to betray their trust—when suddenly, with a shout of "Oh, yes, we are coming!" our loyal little allies fired a volley straight into the midst of the mutineers, killing more than thirty of them, and letting the rebels see that, come what might, the Ghurkas would remain loyal to the salt they had eaten at the Sahibs' hands.

On the 14th of July, an engagement was fought in which our hero came near to ending his life. Roberts, by the means of spies, found out that a more than usually desperate attack was to be made on Hindu Rao's house, which was the keystone of our position on the ridge. "We have beaten them nineteen times, and I don't expect we shall be worsted on the twentieth," cheerfully replied "Ghurka" Reid, when warned of the assault which was to take place.

At eight o'clock in the morning, under shelter of a heavy fire from the city walls, the attack began in earnest. Brigadier Showers was in command. Chamberlain was with him, and Roberts was there as staff officer. Our men—Reid with his Ghurkas in the centre—swept the enemy back. Under the shelter of a low wall the Sepoys clung, and made a desperate resistance. Nothing daunted, Chamberlain, calling to his men to follow, leapt his horse over the wall. He was wounded in doing so; but the British swarmed over, and right up to the walls of Delhi they pursued the flying Sepoys. They pursued them too far, in fact: a murderous fire met them from the city walls;

men were mowed down in scores, and the "retreat" was sounded.

When the retirement began, Roberts was with the two advanced guns. The subaltern in charge of them was severely wounded; the sergeant had fallen with a bullet in his leg. After seeing to the wounded men, all Roberts' attention was turned to saving the guns. The horses, some of them wounded and maddened by the noise and tumult, had become restive and almost unmanageable. As they plunged and reared, Roberts ran to their heads, patted them, and endeavoured to keep them quiet, when, to use his own words, "Suddenly I felt a tremendous blow on my back, which made me faint and sick, and I was afraid I should not be able to remain on my horse." Fortunately the feeling of faintness passed, and he was able to ride back with the retiring guns.

On arrival at camp it was found that he had been struck near the spine by a bullet. By rare good fortune, the leather pouch in which he carried caps for his pistol had slipped round; the bullet struck this, losing its force, and thus the slipping of his belt probably saved our future Field-Marshal's life.

The whole scene was very like that which was enacted many years after under African skies, when, in December 1899, our hero's only son, Lieutenant Roberts, laid down his life at Colenso while gallantly saving the guns. To use the words of Mr. Maclaren Cobban, "Why was there no shifted pouch to save the dear life of the only son?"

This accident kept Roberts on the sick list for a fort-night, and for a month he was unable to wear a sword-belt or to mount a horse. "I remember him well," wrote a doctor who knew him: "a bright, eager little fellow, very cheerful, very even-tempered, with the clear eye and the curious interest of a bird for every detail, and with a decided disposition rather to listen than to talk. He was too young, too quiet and modest, to be a very well-known figure in camp; but with all who did know him he was a great favourite, although none, I imagine, had any notion of the great destiny in store for him."

Before Delhi was once again captured and in British hands, no less than thirty-two fights took place. The struggle was a fierce and desperate one—"a struggle between a mere handful of men along the open ridge, and a host behind massive and well-fortified walls." During this time there had been three officers in chief command. General Barnard had died, stricken by cholera; General Reid was unable to continue at his post, having broken down through strain and anxiety; and it was left to General Wilson to finish the work the others had begun, and finally, in mid-September, to plant the British flag once more on the walls of the ancient city of the Mogul emperors. Wilson had never wavered; from the first he had written, "It is my firm, determination to hold my present position and to resist every attack to the last. The enemy are very numerous, and may possibly break through our entrenchments and overwhelm us, but this force will die at its post."

For some time before the final assault on the city Lieutenant Roberts was especially busy. For a week at a time he never left his battery, except for his meals. While in the battery he had a wonderful escape; he was actually knocked over by a ball and yet remained unhurt.

The British guns were now doing splendid work; night and day they kept firing, and the breaches in the walls began to widen. Late in the afternoon of the 13th, Nicholson, who was to lead the assault, went round the guns to see that all was ready. "He was evidently satisfied," Roberts tells, with pride, "for when he entered our battery he said, 'I must shake hands with you fellows; you have done your best to make my work easy to-morrow.'"

That night there was no work in the batteries; the men lay down and tried to sleep, in view of the hard work before them on the morrow. "Any officer or man who might be wounded was to be left where he fell; no one was to step from the ranks to help him, as there were no men to spare. No prisoners were to be made, as we had no one to guard them; but care was to be taken that no women or children were injured:" so ran the grim orders. Next morning the assault began.

The attacking force was formed in four columns. Roberts, being on the general's staff, was not attached to any of the columns. He, however, rode with the general into the town after our men had gained an entrance, and were desperately fighting their way through the streets. A report that disaster had befallen one of the columns reached the general's staff: Roberts was instantly sent off to find out what had happened. While riding through the Kashmir Gate he saw a doolie without bearers and with a wounded man inside. To quote his own words:—

"I dismounted to see if I could be of any use to the occupant, when I found to my grief and consternation that it was John Nicholson, with death written on his face. He was lying on his back; no wound was visible, and but for the pallor of his face, always colourless, there was no sign of the agony he must have been enduring. On my expressing a hope that he was not seriously wounded, he said, 'I am dying; there is no chance for me.' The sight of that great man lying helpless and on the point of death was almost more than I could bear. Other men had daily died around me, friends and comrades had been killed beside me, *but I never felt as I felt then—to lose Nicholson seemed to me at that moment to lose everything.*"

Nicholson had fallen in the forefront of the battle. With the words, "Come on, men!" on his lips, he had been struck down.

The victory was dearly bought at the cost of this hero's life. "From city to city, from cantonment to cantonment, went the chequered tidings: Delhi had fallen, the King of Delhi was a captive—but John Nicholson was dead."

Delhi was once again in our hands, but fierce fighting still continued in the streets of the city, till on the 10th of

September the palace itself was taken, and for the second time in the century the stronghold of the Moguls was captured by a British force.

Cawnpore and Lucknow

During the siege of Delhi, by his zeal and by the way in which he had never lost an opportunity of serving the cause in which our soldiers were engaged, Roberts had gained much praise from his superior officers. He was "mentioned in dispatches," General Archdale Wilson writing thus: "I beg also to bring very favourably to notice... *that gallant and active officer Lieutenant Roberts.*"

Three days after Delhi had fallen, a force, consisting of 750 British and 1900 native troops, with 16 guns, was sent out, their object being to proceed to Cawnpore, and there join the column which was to advance to the relief of Lucknow.

As the little army left the city, Roberts' heart was full of the saddest feelings, for the funeral of John Nicholson—the great Nicholson Sahib, "the Christian hero, the happy warrior upon whom had come nothing which he did not foresee"—was taking place.

The column had only gone four days on their journey when they met and had a sharp brush with the enemy. In a wild charge for the guns Lieutenant Roberts was the first to reach the enemy's battery. The enemy were driven.

back into the town of Bulandshahr, where some fierce hand-to-hand fighting went on in the narrow streets.

Roberts was riding a somewhat restive horse, a Waziri which had been the favourite of Nicholson. Just in the thickest of the fight a Sepoy took careful aim at our hero. In vain Roberts tried to get at him and cut him down—the throng was too great: the native pulled the trigger and fired point blank. Fortunately, at that instant the charger reared, and received in its own head the bullet which had been meant for its rider. It is pleasant to learn that the faithful Waziri recovered, and bore his master for many a day after.

During the column's advance, the fighting was frequent and continuous. The men were worn thin and lean as greyhounds, so tanned and bronzed by the sun that they looked like natives. They were a terrible, hard-hitting, seasoned force for the enemy to meet, however, and the fame of their doings already inspired terror in the Sepoys' hearts.

At Agra Roberts again had a narrow escape for his life. He was engaged in a single-handed combat with a native. The latter waved his turban in front of the Englishman's charger, and while the startled horse reared back, slashed at its rider. Roberts drew his pistol, but the trigger jammed. His horse refused to come to close quarters, and he could not get near enough the Sepoy to use his own sword. His position was one of extreme danger. At this moment, however, a Lancer galloped up and ran the native through the body.

After leaving Agra, the column were eleven days on the march before they reached Cawnpore. This town, the birthplace of Roberts, was the scene of one of the blackest deeds of the Mutiny. General Wheeler, who was in command there when the wave of mutiny swept over the place, refused to believe in the treachery of his own native troops, with whom he had served for fifty years. His Baba-log (baby-folk) he called them, and he trusted them but too well.

This is not the place to tell the tragedy of Cawnpore, and of the Nana Sahib's treachery. The British force trusted to the Nana's word; they were to leave the city in safety, and be allowed to embark in boats on the river; so he had promised. Scarcely had they pushed off, however, when a murderous fire was directed on them, the boats were set on fire, and many defenceless women and children taken captive. These were confined in one small house to the number of about two hundred. Painfully the days dragged on; at last the guns of Havelock's relieving force were heard. Their troubles, they fondly trusted, were now at an end; but the tiger—the blood-thirsty Nana—was not to be baulked of his prey. Havelock was thrashing his huge Sepoy hosts, and with his handful of men driving them before him. The Nana would at least be avenged on the defenceless women and children he had in his power.

The order to kill went forth. In justice to the Sepoys

they remembered that they were soldiers: their work was to wage war: but, treacherous as they had been to the Sahibs, they revolted at the idea of shooting the Memsahibs and the Baba-log. They obeyed orders to the extent of marching to the prison-house, but there they refused to act; their shots purposely went up into the roof, and no one was hit.

Wild with the passion of cruelty and rage, the Nana now sent hired butchers from the bazaars to do his bidding. No soldierly instincts stayed the hand of these; the work of blood and death went on unchecked by pity, the house became a shambles, and not one escaped the slaughter.

Small wonder that, when Havelock and his Highlanders marched in, a terrible vengeance was enacted. The Highlanders struck terror in the superstitious native mind, and "flying fast, the Nana's troops told everywhere that the Sahibs had come back in strange guise; *some draped like women to remind them what manner of wrong they were sworn to requite.*"

After leaving Cawnpore, Roberts, who at this period seemed to bear a charmed life, had another narrow shave.

While on ahead of the column, accompanied by another officer, looking for a suitable camping-ground, they suddenly found their return barred by a crowd of armed horsemen, who seemed to have sprung from nowhere. They instantly began firing, and bullets were soon whizzing unpleasantly close to the Englishmen's heads. Their only chance of escape lay in riding hard enough to get round the enemy's flank before the Sepoys could stop them.

To use his own words: "Accordingly, we put spurs to our horses, and galloped as fast as they could carry us to our left; the enemy turned in the same direction, and made for the village we must pass, and which we could see was already occupied. The firing got hotter and more uncomfortable as we neared this village, the walls of which we skirted at our best possible pace. We cleared the village, and hoped we had distanced the rebels, when suddenly we came upon a deep *nulla* (a river). Mayne got safely to the other side, but my horse stumbled, and rolled over with me into the water at the bottom. In the fall my hand was slightly cut by my sword, which I had drawn, thinking we might have to fight for our lives; the blood flowed freely, and made the reins so slippery when I tried to remount that it was with considerable difficulty that I got into the saddle. The enemy were already at the edge of the *nulla* and preparing to fire, so there was no time to be lost. I struggled through the water and up the opposite bank, and ducking my head to avoid the shots, now coming thick and fast, galloped straight into some high cultivation in which Mayne had already sought shelter. Finally we succeeded in making our way to the main body of the force, where we found Hope Grant in great anxiety about us, as he had heard the firing and knew we were ahead. The dear old fellow evinced his satisfaction at our safe return by shaking each of us heartily by the hand, repeating over and over again in his quick, quaint way, 'Well, my boys; well, my boys; very glad to have you back! Never thought to see you again.'"

Sir Colin Campbell shortly after this joined the column, which now consisted of about 600 cavalry and 3500 infantry, with 42 guns.

Everything now being ready, the little army set off on its march towards Lucknow. One and all were eager to have a share in the rescue of our suffering countrywomen. Sir Colin had a cheering and inspiriting word to say to each battery and regiment, and the whole force was in grand fighting trim, the Delhi troops, in particular, looking "the picture of workmanlike soldiers."

Roberts was entrusted by Sir Colin, very shortly after this, with the duty of conducting the troops to a large park called the Dilkusha, near Lucknow, where the general intended encamping. He had always a good eye for locality, and he accomplished his work to everybody's satisfaction.

On the 15th November, Roberts had a more than usually hard day of it, and was just looking forward to a long night's sleep, when he was told that the Commander-in-Chief wished to speak to him. On arriving, Sir Colin told him that he thought that there was not enough small-arm ammunition in the camp, and asked Roberts if he could find his way back in the dark to the "Alumbagh," a large bungalow passed on the march, in which the cartridges had been stored. "I am sure I can," came the ready answer.

Accompanied by two other officers, Roberts meant to start with a guide; the latter, however, soon bolted, and the little party had now to trust to our lieutenant entirely for its safety. It was an exciting night. First there was the risk of coming upon the enemy—indeed, several times they were dangerously near the Sepoy piquets; then, again, there was the chance that our men in the "Alumbagh" might mistake them for the foe, and fire upon them. Roberts left his companions and rode on alone. The sentry challenged immediately, but after some parleying he gained the bungalow and explained what he wanted. The lading up was quickly finished, and by dawn the ammunition was, as Sir Colin had ordered, safe in our soldiers' hands at Lucknow. Old Sir Colin, only half-dressed, greeted the escort most heartily, and warmly praised Roberts, who describes his old Chief's welcome and approval as "a very happy moment."

That same day the troops moved forward, and after some days' hard fighting the object of the expedition was achieved, and the women and children, and the brave garrison, were able to march out in safety and join the attacking column.

Before entrance to the city could be made, our guns had to batter a breach in the walls. At last a hole three feet square and three feet from the ground was made. It was a small opening through which to storm a town, but Sir Colin determined on the attack.

The order was given, and then started a wild rush.

"It was a magnificent sight, a sight never to be forgotten," says Roberts, "that glorious struggle to be the first to enter the deadly breach, the prize to the winner of the race being certain death! Highlanders and Sikhs, Punjabi Mahommedans, Dogras and Pathans, all vied with each other in the generous competition. A Highlander was the first to reach the goal, and was shot dead as he jumped into the enclosure; a man of the 4th Punjab Infantry came next, and met the same fate. Then followed Lieutenant Cooper, of the 93rd, and immediately behind him his colonel (Ewart), Captain Lumsden, of the 30th Bengal Infantry, and a number of Sikhs and Highlanders, as fast as they could scramble through the opening. A drummer-boy of the 93rd must have been one of the first to pass that grim boundary between life and death, for when I got in I found him just inside the breach, lying on his back quite dead— a pretty, innocent-looking, fair-haired lad, not more than fourteen years of age."

Once our troops had poured through the breach, the enemy were completely taken by surprise, and caught in a trap. Two thousand of them had collected in a sort of large courtyard, intending to assault our flanks. Into this courtyard, however, our men dashed. The Sepoys had no outlet but a single gateway and the breach we had made. Escape was not to be thought of; the rebels fought to sell their lives as dearly as they could; no mercy, they knew, awaited the slayers of women and children. Inch by inch they were forced back to the pavilion, and bayoneted and shot down till not a man remained. The Sahibs had delayed their vengeance, but it was swift and terrible when it did come.

Next day the troops were at it again. The first object to be gained was the mess-house, on which our guns were soon merrily pounding. Sir Colin, who sat on his white horse watching the attack, as soon as the mess-house was captured bade Roberts hoist our flag on the top, to show the beleaguered garrison the success of the arms coming to their aid. Assisted by two other officers, Roberts planted the standard of the loyal 2nd Punjabis on the loftiest turret. Twice was the standard shot away, and twice did the gallant lieutenant, amid a storm of bullets, replace it. Again it fell, the staff this time broken in two. Once more Roberts picked up the colour and managed to prop it up a third time on the turret, where it remained at last, a sight to cheer the loyal garrison and strike terror into the hearts of the rebels.

At last the "Relief" was accomplished and the brave defenders rescued. Unable to take the city with the small force available, rescuers and rescued retired.

Roberts, who seemed to have a genius for finding his way in the dark, was, as night fell, sent with a message to General Hale, to tell him at what time the troops were to withdraw. Having delivered this message in safety, in spite of the dangers around him, Roberts returned to join the main body. To his dismay he found the positions we had gained, deserted. The whole force had moved off and he was alone—the one Englishman in Lucknow! The experience was a trying one, but Roberts was used to danger, and calmly turning his horse's head from the city, he galloped on the line of route his instinct told him our army had followed.

Fortunately for him the enemy had not discovered that the British had stolen away, and after a hard gallop he reached the straggling column in safety.

For days the work had been desperately severe, and arrived at the "Alumbâgh"—the villa from which he had got the ammunition—Roberts had the first wash and change of clothes during ten days' fighting.

Despite the never-ending work, the brief snatches of sleep, and the fact that he almost lived on horseback, Roberts described himself as very fit and in splendid training. He was now all eagerness for more fighting, and started in high spirits for the march on Cawnpore, where he was to win what every soldier prizes above any other honour, "The Victoria Cross."

The End of the Mutiny

On the 27th December the column started from Lucknow to go to the relief of Cawnpore.

Roberts had no light work before him in arranging the transport for such an unwieldy army as the force had now become. The column, with all its train, extended from ten to twelve miles in length, and frequently its head had reached the end of the day's journey before its tail was ready to start. The next day heavy firing was heard in the direction of Cawnpore, and a native met the force with a note, written in Greek characters, addressed to Sir Colin, "or any officer commanding troops on the Lucknow road." This letter told of the sore straits the troops at Cawnpore were in, and urgently begged that help might be sent as soon as possible.

The news acted like magic on the tired, straggling troops. To use the words of an eye-witness, who published the account shortly afterwards, "the impatience and anxiety of all became extreme. Louder and louder grew the roar; faster and faster became the march; long and weary was the way; tired and footsore grew the infantry; death fell on the exhausted wounded with terrible rapidity; the travel-worn bearers could hardly stagger along under their loads; the sick men groaned and died—but still on, on, on was the cry." Sir Colin was in a fever of impatience, and anxious lest the bridge of boats which led to the city had been destroyed. Roberts was sent on ahead to find whether this was the case or not, and great was the rejoicing when he returned, bearing the news that the bridge was still undestroyed. The passage over the boats was, however, a long and tedious job, and it took from 3 p.m. on the 29th till about 9 p.m. the next day before the last of the troops had safely crossed.

The time had now come to read the mutineers in Cawnpore a lesson.

Lord Roberts writes: "Sunday, the 6th December, was one of those glorious days in which the European in Northern India revels for a great part of the winter—clear and cool, with a cloudless sky. I awoke refreshed, after a good night's rest, and in high spirits at the prospect before us of a satisfactory day's work; for we hoped to drive the enemy from Cawnpore, and to convince those who had witnessed—if not taken part in—the horrible brutalities there, *that England's hour had come at last.*"

Sir Colin, whose little army had been lately reinforced by the arrival of the 42nd, the famous Black Watch, had now a force of about 5000 infantry, 600 cavalry, and 35 guns.

The rebel army consisted of 25,000 men, with 40 guns, so the odds against the British were very great. But a desperate courage ran through the whole of Sir Colin's force, and weight of numbers mattered little to the spirit of daring, and the just desire for vengeance, which possessed our men.

Roberts describes the advance as a "sight to be remembered." Across a grassy plain the British moved steadily onwards, marching as though on parade, despite the storm of shot which plunged through them, or ricocheted over their heads.

The loyal 4th Punjabis, supported by the 53rd Foot, were the first to charge the rebels. Native soldier and British fought side by side with fierce valour, and soon the Sepoys broke, and fled across the canal.

Soon after the attack, Sir Colin Campbell and Sir Hope Grant (Roberts, of course, accompanying them), with their respective staffs, hurried up and joined in the fight. The rebel camp was soon broken up, and orders were given for a pursuit. By some accident the mounted troops were not yet up. The rebels must not be allowed to escape without further punishment. Sir Colin was not long in doubt. Supported by Bourchier's battery, he determined to follow them up himself, with only his escort.

"What a chase we had!" says Roberts. "We went at a gallop, only pulling up occasionally for the battery to come into action, to clear our front and flanks."

For two miles did the chase continue without a check, when a halt was called. While the horses were having a breather, the cavalry came up, and off they all started again, Sir Colin taking the lead, the mutineers bolting in all directions.

"The pursuit is continued to the fourteenth milestone, assuming all the character of a fox-hunt. Strange to say, not many miles beyond the enemy's camp, a fox broke right in front of the enemy, and a view-halloa told Reynard that the heavy crops would be his safest refuge. At the fourteenth mile-stone, on the banks of the Pandoo river, the pursuit ceased, not a trace either of an enemy or a cart of any kind being in sight."

The defeat of the enemy was complete, and when Roberts rode his weary steed back, in order to select a camping-ground in front of Cawnpore, the rebel army had ceased to exist. Such as had not been cut down in the chase had thrown away their arms, and were for the future as harmless as the innocent peasants they pretended to be.

Part of the Cawnpore force, indeed—those who had been within the city—had escaped, and to Roberts the duty fell of finding out where they had gone. This, with the help of a trusty native guide, he was soon able to do, and the rebels were overtaken and speedily routed, with the loss of all their guns.

Two days before Christmas, the British again moved forward, in order to restore order, and open up the roads between Bengal and the Punjab. On New Year's Day (1858) the troops were halted near Futtehghur, as the enemy had turned, and seemed determined to make a stand. Their courage was, however, gone. Our men, flushed with victory, charged the Sepoys with a will. "Then despair seized upon the rebel mass; breaking their ranks, throwing aside their arms, they fled in wild confusion; but the horsemen were upon them and amongst them. The slaughter was terrible; for several miles they rode along, spearing and cutting down at every step."

The chase continued till daylight began to fall: the fugitives seemed all to have been dispersed, and our men were ordered to form up in the road. To describe the ensuing incident we shall use Roberts' own words:—

"Before, however, this movement could be carried out, we overtook a batch of mutineers, who faced about and fired into the squadron at close quarters. I saw Younghusband fall, but I could not go to his assistance, as at that moment one of his '*sowers*' was in dire peril from a Sepoy who was attacking him with his fixed bayonet, and had I not helped the man and disposed of his opponent, he must have been killed. The next moment I descried in the distance two Sepoys making off with a standard, which I determined must be captured, so I rode after the rebels and overtook them, and, while wrenching the staff out of the hands of one of them, whom I cut down, the other put his musket close to my body and fired; fortunately for me it missed fire, and I carried off the standard."

In such simple language does our great soldier tell the story of a deed of bravery and courage which bore with it its reward—a reward more valued than any other our soldiers can attain.

"For these two acts I was awarded the Victoria Cross," is how Lord Roberts modestly puts it in a footnote to his book, "Forty-one Years in India."

Nearly a month was spent at Futtehghur, after which the force was kept busy clearing the country and keeping the roads open. While engaged in this duty, Roberts was one day out for a ride with a brother officer. He was followed by a greyhound, which always accompanied its master. Suddenly a "nilghai," or antelope, got up in front of them, so close that Roberts' brother officer aimed a blow at it with his sword and gashed its quarter. Off started the greyhound after the quarry, and the two eager riders were soon galloping in the chase as hard as their horses could go.

Suddenly they saw moving towards them a large body of the enemy's cavalry. Their horses were blown after their long gallop, and escape seemed impossible. Thinking their last hour had come, the two young Englishmen shook hands and said "good-bye," determined at the worst to sell their lives dearly. "When lo! as suddenly as they appeared, the horsemen vanished, as though the ground had opened and swallowed them; there was nothing to be seen but the open plain, where a second before there had been a crowd of mounted men." The whole thing was in reality an illusion, or mirage, so well known to travellers in the desert.

There now remained the last act in the Mutiny. This was the siege and final capture of Lucknow, and here, from the 2nd to the 21st of March, when the city fell, Roberts was actively engaged. The rebels fought with the courage of despair, and offered a splendid resistance, in which numbers of the Highlanders and Punjabis fell. Hodson, of Hodson's Horse, was killed, to the sorrow of the whole British force. He had shot with his own hand the rebel sons of the King of Delhi, for which act he has been blamed. But his unflinching courage and personal bravery won him the respect and admiration of all soldiers; and loyal natives and British alike mourned the early death of their daring leader.

The hard work and all he had gone through had told on Roberts, but, with the fall of Lucknow, the fighting was practically over.

On the 1st of April 1858, six years after his arrival in India, he handed over the office of Deputy-Assistant-Quarter-Master-General to another soldier, who has become likewise famous as Viscount Wolseley, and towards the middle of the month he left Lucknow.

Before leaving, Sir Colin Campbell thanked him for his services, and promised at the earliest opportunity to give him the rank of brevet-major.

Thus, having won golden opinions from his superior officers, and "having during his first half-dozen years in India seen more of fighting than many soldiers see in lifetime," Lieutenant Roberts, on May 4th, embarked on the P. & O. *Nubia* on his way to England and home.

Marriage—At Home—Return to India—The Lushai Expedition—Abyssinia

The young Mutiny hero had a very pleasant voyage home, travelling overland through Europe by way of Trieste, Venice, and Switzerland, and arriving in England in the end of June. "The intense delight of getting home after one's first term of exile can hardly be exaggerated, and certainly cannot be realised save by those who have gone through the exile, and been separated, as I had been, for years, from all that made the happiness of my early life," writes Lord Roberts. "Every English tree and flower one comes across on first landing is a distinct and lively pleasure, while the greenness and freshness are a delicious rest to the eye, wearied with the deadly whitey-brown sameness of dried-up, sandy plains, or the all too gorgeous colouring of eastern cities and pageants."

His people were living in Ireland, in the county of Waterford, and General Roberts, wonderfully hale and hearty in spite of his seventy-four years (fifty of which had been spent in India), was greatly delighted to welcome his son home again, and to hear from his own lips all that so deeply interested the veteran concerning the tragedy of the Mutiny.

Roberts was a fearless horseman, and many a good run did he have during the winter with Lord Waterford's hounds, the famous "Curraghmore." While on leave, Roberts met Miss Norah Bews, whom he married on the 17th May 1859, the ceremony taking place in the parish church of Waterford, which was most gaily decorated for the occasion.

The honeymoon was spent in Scotland, and was interrupted by a command from the Queen for Roberts to be present at Buckingham Palace on the 8th June, in order to receive at her Majesty's hands the decoration of the Victoria Cross.

On the 27th June, little more than a month after their wedding, the newly-married couple started for India.

The heat in the Red Sea was appalling, hotter even than on Roberts' first trip, and to make matters worse they encountered a terrific storm in the Indian Ocean. To quote Lord Roberts: "Eventually we arrived in Calcutta, in rather a dilapidated condition, on the 30th July."

Roberts was soon actively employed. The dominions which had been formerly ruled by the East India Company were to be formally taken over by the Queen. To celebrate this event the Viceroy, Lord Canning, made a great triumphal tour, "a six-months' march over a thousand miles," and to Roberts fell the duty of organising this huge pageant.

Mrs. Roberts accompanied her husband on this tour. Lucknow was their first halt. We can well imagine with what interest the young couple went over the places, now quiet and peaceful, which had but a short time before been the scenes of so much violence and bloodshed.

"I made use of the next week," writes Roberts, "which was for me a comparatively idle time, to take my wife over the ground by which we had advanced two years before, and explain to her the different positions held by the enemy. She was intensely interested in visiting the Sikandarbagh, the Shah Najaf, the mess-house, and, above all, that glorious memorial of almost super-human courage and endurance, the Residency, mined, roofless, and riddled by round shot and bullets."

After his duty with the Viceroy was ended, Roberts, his wife, and their little daughter, who was born on March 10th, went to Simla. Here, in a glorious climate, they lived in a bungalow well named Mount Pleasant, which was approached through a forest of rhododendron, along a path crimson with fallen blossom. Both were delighted with their new quarters. "Our servants had arranged everything in our little abode most comfortably; bright fires were burning in the grates, a cosy breakfast was awaiting us, and the feeling that at last we had a home of our own was very pleasant."

Lieutenant Roberts' promotion, when it came, burst

with surprising rapidity. When the East India Company's army became joined to the Queen's forces he got his step; on 12th November 1860 he became a captain; the following day his name appeared in the *Gazette* as a brevet-major!

This year he had again the management of the Viceroy's camp, but this was on a much smaller scale than the year before. During the Viceroy's progress Roberts had plenty of shooting, and on this occasion shot his first tiger.

"Not considering myself a first-rate shot," he says, in his usual modest way, "I thought I should be best employed with the beaters; but, as good luck would have it, the tiger broke from the jungle within a few yards of my elephant; I could not resist having a shot, and was fortunate enough to knock him over."

Roberts had been disappointed in not being sent with the expedition to China, with whom we were then at war. His old chief, Sir Colin Campbell, now Lord Clyde, had thought it hardly fair to send off a newly-married man so far on such a dangerous mission, and was much surprised that both the young major and his wife should not be more grateful to him for having spared them the separation. When Mrs. Roberts told him how sorry they both were at his having to stay behind, the old Scotsman burst out in his rough, half-playful way: "Well, I'll be hanged if I can understand you women! I have done the very thing I thought you would like, and have only succeeded in making you angry. I will never try to help a woman again."

Though he was not to take part in the fighting in China, Roberts had his chance nearer home, towards the end of 1865.

As usual, there was trouble on the frontier. Many of the rebels who had escaped the Mutiny had fled over the border, and with the aid of fanatics were continually stirring up the tribes to revolt. In order to check this disturbance General Garvock was despatched with a force of about five thousand men. Major Roberts was with the mountain battery which led the way, and was in the thick of the two days' fighting which followed, and in which the tribes were completely beaten. The terms of peace were that the Bunerwals should go and destroy the village of the fanatics who had made all the trouble. This they consented to do, and Roberts and six other officers went with them to see the agreement carried out.

It was a dangerous job for the little band of Englishmen. The villagers looked on in sulky silence as their homes were set on fire. There was deep anger in their hearts towards the hated white men who were the cause of the deed, and who now stood amongst them.

Murmurs at last led to threats of violence; the tribesmen began to crowd round Roberts and his dauntless companions. At this moment the staunchness of the Bunerwals probably saved their lives. "You are hesitating whether you will allow these English to return unmolested," broke in an old, grey-bearded chief. "You can, of course, murder them and their escort, but if you do you must kill us Bunerwals first, for we have sworn to protect them, and we will do so with our lives." The little band returned in safety, though they had had a narrow escape for their lives: and on his return to Simla Roberts found his wife had been most anxious for his safety. She had accidentally heard the expedition described as "madness" by Sir Hugh Rose, the Commander-in-Chief. "It was madness, and not one of them will ever come back alive," he had said while passing her tent. We can well imagine with what delight she hailed her husband's return, as, till the morning of the day he returned, she had had no news of his safety.

Shortly after this, Major Roberts was ordered home on sick leave, and with his wife he sailed in February, on board a transport, for the long voyage round the Cape.

His first action at the inspection parade on board ship was to let off all the culprits detailed for punishment. He addressed the men in a few short, manly sentences, told them that he was unwilling to commence their acquaintance by awarding punishments, and that he hoped their future conduct would show him that he had not made a mistake in being too lenient.

"The officers seemed somewhat surprised at my action in this matter," says Roberts, "but I think it was proved by the men's subsequent conduct that I had not judged them incorrectly, for they all behaved in quite an exemplary manner throughout the voyage."

After a few months at home Major Roberts again sailed

for India, in March. In that year a brigade was sent from Bengal to Abyssinia. The king of the country, Theodore, had ill-treated and imprisoned some Europeans, and it was determined to punish him. Roberts was chosen, much to his delight, to go with the troops as Assistant-Quartermaster-General, and on the 3rd of February they anchored in Annerly Bay, near Zula, a port of Abyssinia.

He was not, however, to take part in the fighting, but had to remain as senior staff officer and look after the transport arrangements. The heat was almost unbearable, 117° in Major Roberts' tent. Roberts was very fortunate in finding an old friend and Eton schoolfellow on duty in the harbour. This was Captain Tryon, afterwards Admiral Sir George Tryon, K.C.B., whose untimely end, many years afterwards, in the sinking of H.M.S. *Victoria*, plunged the whole nation into mourning. To his old schoolfellow, our hero tells us, he owed many a good dinner, and, what I appreciated even more, many a refreshing bath on board the *Euphrates*"—a transport fitted up for Captain Tryon and his staff.

For four months Roberts stayed in the furnace heat of Zula. On the 17th April news came that Magdala had fallen, and the object of the expedition was accomplished.

On the 2nd June Sir Robert Napier, Commander-in-Chief, returned to Zula, and on the 10th he embarked for home, taking Roberts with him as his bearer of final despatches.

On his arrival home Roberts was met by his wife, and on

the 14th of August, among the rewards for the Abyssinian Expedition, his name appeared for a brevet lieutenant-colonelcy. On January 4, 1869, Colonel Roberts, with his wife and child, again left for India. On the voyage they experienced the great sorrow of losing their little girl, who died on board ship, and was buried at sea.

The next two years were spent quietly at Simla, in a round of official duties. Among other things, Colonel Roberts went through a course of electric telegraphy, and was soon able to send and to receive messages on the instrument. In the summer of 1871 there again was a chance of active service for the young colonel.

In the district round Cachar, between South-eastern Bengal and Burma, it was found that the tea-plant would thrive to an extraordinary degree. Gradually the jungles became cleared, and the tea-gardens were pushed further and further into what had been but lately the wilds.

The native tribe, the Lushais, whose territory was thus encroached upon, were a wild, fierce people. From time to time they had raided the tea-gardens, done the planters much damage, and carried off prisoners. Small expeditions had been sent out to punish them; but, from various causes, these had not met with much success. The Lushais became bolder, raids on the gardens became more frequent, until at last the raiders kidnapped the daughter of a planter, a little girl named Mary Winchester.

It was then thought that the time for action had come, and this was absolutely necessary for the future security of British subjects. Two columns were therefore fitted out, and Colonel Roberts was appointed as chief staff officer, his orders being "to fit out and despatch the two columns and then join General Bourchier at Cachar."

The progress of the columns was slow; the way lay through a dense jungle with thick undergrowth, and at times the men could only march in single file. At one time the road was "blocked by a curious erection in the form of a gallows, from which hung two grotesque figures made of bamboos." "A little further on it was a felled tree which stopped us; this tree was studded all over with knife-like pieces of bamboos, and from the incisions into which these were stuck exuded a red juice, exactly the colour of blood. This was the Lushais' mode of warning us what would be our fate if we ventured further."

After some fighting, the tribe saw that the Government was in earnest, and soon came to terms.

On New Year's Day 1872, Colonel Roberts received the news that he had gained an important step in his department, and had been appointed Deputy-Quartermaster-General. A few days later he got the news of the birth of a son and heir at Umballa. Though there had not been much fighting, the expedition had had a trying time, marching in the jungle and subsisting mainly on tinned foods, and no one was sorry when peace was made and the troops were able to return. For his services against the Lushais Colonel Roberts received the C.B.

For the next four or five years Colonel Roberts was to

spend a life of duty and routine without actual fighting. He had much to do with making the arrangements for the Prince of Wales' successful tour in India in 1875.

Again, in January 1877, he was kept busy in forming the huge camp at Delhi when, amid much pomp and ceremony, the Queen was proclaimed Empress of India.

Shortly after, events in Afghanistan began to look threatening, and Roberts was soon to find a wider field for his military genius.

Afghanistan

On the 15th March 1878, Roberts took up the command of the Punjab Frontier Force. He had often longed for a command, and the Frontier Force promised chances for active service afforded by no other post.

Events in Afghanistan were now coming to a crisis, and it was proposed to send a mission to try to come to terms and settle all disputes. Accordingly, an Englishman, Major Cavagnari, was told to go to Kabul and. let the Amir know that a mission would soon arrive.

Major Cavagnari had, however, hardly crossed the frontier when he was met by the Afghan general, Faiz Mahomed. Faiz Mahomed treated the English officer courteously, but told him distinctly that he had orders not to let the mission pass. Such was the command of his master the Amir; nay more, "but for their personal friendship," he said, "he would, in obedience to further orders from the treacherous Afghan ruler, have shot Major Cavagnari down, and his escort." This direct insult could not be allowed to pass unnoticed. The peaceful mission was forced to retire, but to take its place two British columns were immediately formed, and the command of one of these columns—the Kuram Field Force—was given to Major-General Roberts.

The object of this force was to defeat and disperse any Afghan army that might march to oppose it, and at the same time it was to threaten Kabul, and thus try and bring the Amir to his senses.

On the 21st of November our troops crossed the frontier, General Roberts being in front with the advanced guard. As the British advanced the Afghans sullenly retired, and finally took up a very strong position on a hill called the Peiwar Kotal. The general had only a small force with him (it consisted of 1345 British and 3990 native soldiers, with 13 guns), but he determined to strike a blow.

The tribes in the Kurman thought the small army doomed. "Even the women taunted us," says Roberts. "When they saw the little Gurkhas for the first time, they exclaimed, 'Is it possible that these beardless boys think they can fight Afghan warriors?' They little suspected that the brave spirits which animated these small forms made them more than a match for the most stalwart Afghan."

The plan of attack was soon formed. It was to make a night march, arrive at the foot of the Kotal Hill, where the enemy lay encamped, and storm the position by daybreak. Meanwhile the Afghans' attention was turned to every point of assault but the one determined on.

With great skill the general made use of his small forces by spreading them out, and feinting to attack in different places. In consequence of this, the enemy were completely puzzled and out-manœuvred.

At 10 p.m. on Sunday the 1st December, the men fell in, and began their perilous march in absolute silence. A bitterly cold wind blew down the valley, and by the fitful moonlight, over boulders and through mountain torrents, the soldiers surely but steadily toiled upwards. As dawn was breaking, the enemy saw them, and hastily began to fire into them. Up leapt the Gurkhas and Highlanders, and side by side charged wildly into the entrenchments. A fierce hand-to-hand fight followed; the Afghans fought bravely, but after a short resistance the plateau was taken, and the enemy fled.

Roberts, who led the attack in person, had a narrow escape, a bullet whistling past him, and actually grazing his finger. During the thickest of the fight his native orderlies showed the greatest devotion to their well-loved master. He had two Sikhs, two Pathans, and two Gurkhas in attendance on him, and while the firing was at its hottest, all six crowded round him, regardless of their own safety, as long as they could shield the general from the storm of bullets.

After two hours' well-earned rest, the troops again marched forward on the enemy's main position. The attack on the enemy's front had also been successful, and soon the whole Afghan camp was in our soldiers' hands. The foe were in headlong flight, pursued by our cavalry. The rout was complete; their guns, waggons, and baggage were left behind, and General Roberts had won his maiden victory.

The victorious general now made all his plans for a march on Kabul as soon as spring came. News came, however, that a treaty of peace had been signed, and that a peaceful British mission was to be sent to the Amir's capital. On hearing this, Roberts bade farewell to his splendid little army, and started off to return to Simla. Before actually leaving, he met the Peace Mission, which consisted of Major Cavagnari, who was accompanied by three other Englishmen, and an escort of the Guides.

They were all in the best of spirits, but General Roberts was haunted by a feeling of approaching disaster. At dinner he sat silent, filled "with gloomy forebodings as to the fate of those fine fellows." Next morning he rode with them part of the way. A solitary magpie—emblem of bad luck—flew past them, and Major Cavagnari begged the general not to tell his wife of their ill-omened start. With a heavy heart Roberts bade the little company good-bye. "My heart sank," says he, "as I wished Cavagnari good-bye. When we proceeded a few yards in our different directions, we both turned round, retraced our steps, shook hands once more, *and parted for ever.*"

This parting took place in July; between one and two on the morning of the 5th September, Roberts—who had returned to Simla—was awakened by the arrival of a telegram. The contents told him that his worst fears were realised. Cavagnari and his comrades had been treacherously murdered in the Residency at Kabul.

This, of course, meant war; the murderers must be punished, the murdered mission avenged. With the least possible delay, Roberts was soon busily engaged in plans for the formation of "The Kabul Field Force," as his new command was called.

On the 6th of September he left Simla and went to Umballa, where he was joined by his staff. When he reached the troops the general received a most hearty and enthusiastic welcome, and he was much cheered by the bearing of his soldiers.

"A splendid spirit pervaded the whole force; the men's hearts were on fire with eager desire to press on to Kabul, and be led against the miscreants who had foully murdered our countrymen, and I felt assured that whatever it was possible for dauntless courage, unselfish devotion, and firm determination to achieve, would be achieved by my gallant soldiers."

The troops moved steadily on. On the 5th of October, exactly a month after the sad news of the fate of Cavagnari had reached Simla, it was halted at the "pretty little village of Charasia, nestling in orchards and gardens, with a rugged range of hills towering above it, about a mile away."

The general had made up his mind to strike while the iron was hot. The Afghans were in great numbers, and strongly posted; they were being hourly reinforced, and the situation was one of great anxiety. After breakfast the attack began: delay might have been fatal; and Roberts, grasping the situation at a glance, hurled his little force straight at the dense hordes of Afghans on the ridge.

The enemy were obstinate, and fought with dogged courage. The ground was steep and difficult, and the advance of the stalwart Highlanders was somewhat checked in consequence. Seeing this dilemma, their brother hill-men (the little Gurkhas) joined them, with the fierce, active Punjabis. Highlanders, Gurkhas, Punjabis, all men of fighting race, united in a desperate charge.

Loading and firing as steadily as if on parade, our troops went on till finally the position was reached, and cold steel was called upon to do its work. The Afghans fought well, but the attack was not to be resisted, and finally they fled, leaving their trenches in the hands of our gallant troops.

The order for a general advance was now sounded, and Highlanders, Gurkhas, and Punjabis again dashed forward in friendly rivalry, each striving hard to be the first to close with the enemy.

The Afghans could not meet their fierce onslaught: first they wavered, then, finally, they scattered and fled in all directions, and the victory was won.

A day or two afterwards the victorious army were at Kabul: the city was at their mercy, and so far their success had been complete. Though the entry into Kabul had been accomplished there was still much to be done. The murderers of Cavagnari had to be brought to justice, order had to be kept in the city, and all the plans made for the army's going into winter quarters.

While in the city Roberts visited the spot where the members of the Residency had made their brave defence and met their cruel end. He was familiar with such scenes of native treachery and British courage; and doubtless the scene of Cavagnari's last stand must have brought back to the Mutiny hero the days of Delhi, Cawnpore, and Lucknow.

"The walls of the Residency, closely pitted with bullet holes, gave proof of the determined nature of the attack and the length of the resistance. The floors were covered with blood-stains, and amidst the embers of a fire were found a heap of human bones. It may be imagined how British soldiers' hearts burned within them at such a sight, and how difficult it was to suppress feelings of hatred and animosity towards the perpetrators of such a dastardly crime."

In the meantime, although the British army was in Kabul, it was by no means in safety, nor was the war at an end. The 8th December saw the enemy's "last peaceful act." That day a great parade of all the troops was held in order to show the Afghans "our teeth and our mettle." Six days after, the enemy had become so daring that General Roberts got all his troops together within the Sharpur Cantonments. Two days before Christmas the Afghans made their fiercest attack. This was beaten back by the steady courage of our troops, who, surrounded by masses of the enemy, and in the heart of a hostile country, were now fighting for their very existence.

The weather was bitterly cold; there was a very hard frost, and the ground was covered thick with snow. "I think I had good reason to be proud of my force," says Roberts. "Native and European soldiers alike bore the hardships and the exposure with the utmost cheerfulness, and in perfect confidence that when the assault should take place victory should be ours."

On the 5th of May Sir Donald Stewart arrived with his force, having marched from Kandahar and gained a great victory on the way. Sir Donald, as senior officer, took command of the united forces. The army was divided into three divisions, Roberts retaining the command of two divisions.

With such a large army in front of Kabul it was thought that some of the troops might be sent back. Accordingly a column was formed, the command of which was given to Roberts, and the idea was that the little army should withdraw by the Kurman route.

Roberts himself had started off in order to view the Khyber Pass, when in his own words: "Suddenly a presentiment, which I have never been able to explain to myself, made me retrace my steps and hurry back towards Kabul—a presentiment of coming trouble."

This feeling, as in the case of Cavagnari, was justified; as, on approaching Kabul, he was met by Sir Donald

Stewart with the news of a grave disaster to the British arms. This was the defeat of General Burrows' force at Maiwand.

The general had left Kandahar with about 2500 men, and on reaching Maiwand the little army had been attacked by 25,000 Afghans. The artillery stood to their guns till all their ammunition had been fired away. Our troops fought doggedly, but they were overwhelmed by numbers, and were finally broken. Nearly half the British force was killed, wounded, or missing; the remnant struggled on through the night, and reached Kandahar the next morning. General Burrows, who in the fight had two horses shot under him, was among the last to reach the city.

Kandahar was soon besieged, a vast native army hemming in the British force.

The consequences of this defeat might well be expected to be serious and far-reaching. "The disaster to our arms caused, as was to be expected, considerable excitement all along the border; indeed throughout India the announcement produced a feeling of uneasiness—a mere surface ripple, but enough to make those who remembered the days of the Mutiny anxious for better news from the north."

Roberts was quick to grasp the situation. He saw that a force ought, without delay, to be sent from Kabul to the relief of Kandahar. After consulting with General Stewart, he sent a telegram to the Adjutant-General in India, in which he told his views plainly and to the point.

"I strongly recommend that a force be sent from this to Kandahar," he began. *"You need have no fears about my division. It can take care of itself, and will reach Kandahar under the month,"* he continued.

On the 3rd of August the reply came; the authorities cordially agreed, and an assent was given.

Roberts was given a free hand in selecting his troops, and he quickly chose an army of close on 10,000 men, with 18 guns. All sorts of fighting men were represented, and many nationalities—Highlanders, British Lancers, British Artillery, with Sikhs, Punjabis, Gurkhas, Native Cavalry, and Native Artillery.

On the 9th of August, at 6 a.m., the force bade farewell to Kabul, and started on its famous march. From that date till its triumphant entry into Kandahar "Sir Frederick Roberts' army was cut off from all communication with India and the outer world." Of this historic march, with its record of heroism, of dangers met, and difficulties overcome, this is not the place to tell.

The picked troops marched splendidly. The general, ever anxious for the comfort and safety of his men, had arranged the whole scheme with absolute fearlessness and prudent forethought.

To quote from the words of an officer who was with the column: "While it must be allowed that the whole force, men and officers, had done their duty nobly, and had accomplished a march which has seldom been surpassed, still the key of the movement was the firm determination of the general commanding. Few commanders have been more personally liked by all, from the drummer to the colonel, than was General Roberts; and the national and universal admiration which this march and subsequent victory inspired, has stamped it as one of the greatest achievements of the British army."

All ranks believed and trusted in their leader, and though the work was hard, the way long and weary, one and all would have fallen on the march rather than give in.

On the morning of the 31st the force reached Kandahar, having marched just over 313 miles from Kabul. Next morning the battle was fought. The fighting was of a fierce and often hand-to-hand order. On the British dashed, position after position being carried at the point of the bayonet. "Just one charge more to close the business!" Major White shouted as he led his men at an intrenchment, and in this spirit of reckless gaiety and daring officers and men alike fought. Soon the foe were in confusion, and, with comparatively slight loss on our side, the Afghans were utterly routed, and Kandahar and the besieged force relieved.

Peace was soon afterwards made, all the British demands being fully satisfied, and the victorious general started to return to India, his work nobly done and ended. "I shall never forget the feeling of sadness with which I said good-bye to the men who had done so much for me," says Roberts. "I looked upon them all, Native as well as British, as my valued friends. And well I might, for never had a commander been better served."

With the ringing cheers of the soldiers he had led to victory, and the pathetic strains of "Auld lang syne" in his ears, Roberts bade farewell to the gallant army which had made his name and its own so famous, and started off for Quetta, on his way to England.

Return to India—South African War—Conclusion

When Sir Frederick Roberts landed in England on November 17, 1880, he found himself the hero of the hour. Honours fell thick upon him; for his services in Afghanistan he was created a Baronet, received the thanks of both Houses of Parliament, and was appointed to the command of the army of Madras.

The march to Kandahar had aroused the greatest excitement and fired the popular imagination, and vast crowds met to cheer the general who, amid so many trials and dangers, had led his army to victory.

His well-earned rest at home was, however, to be but short.

On Sunday, 27th February 1881, came the news of the defeat of the British arms under General Colley by the Boers at Majuba Hill.

On Monday Roberts was asked to take command of the army which was assembling in Natal in order to avenge this defeat. In the short space of five days the general—"ready, aye ready for the field "—had sailed with his staff from Southampton.

As we know, the time for "wiping something off a slate" had not yet come, owing to the strange policy of the British Government. Roberts himself describes how he was sent on "a wild-goose chase." The ship had no sooner entered Table Bay than a telegram was handed to him which ordered him to return at once, as a peace had been patched up, and there was no further need of his services. His stay at Cape Town was indeed limited to twenty-four hours. "The Government seemed to be as anxious to get him away as they had been to hurry him out there."

After a short time at home he again set sail for India, in order to take up the command of the Madras army. This army was much improved during the time General Roberts was at its head. The Madrassi is often a tall, finely set-up, handsome man. In the days of Clive, and even later, he had shown himself a bold fighter, but years of peace had left their mark on him. In spite of his imposing appearance on parade, Roberts saw that the ordinary Southern Indian, as a fighting-man, is "soft."

Still he did not despair of him; he was as a rule better educated and more intelligent than the warlike native of the north. Accordingly the general determined to create an enthusiasm for marksmanship and rifle-practice among the troops. He himself set the example by becoming a keen rifle shot, and he was well backed up in this interest by his staff, among whom was Captain Hamilton, now General Sir Ian Hamilton.

In July 1885, on the retirement of Sir Donald Stewart, Sir Frederick Roberts succeeded to the proud position of Commander-in-Chief in India. During the seven years he held this post, Roberts won the esteem, admiration, and affection of all, Native and European, from the highest to the lowest. Under his command many important improvements in the condition of the army were made; and he brought all his skill and experience to bear on the question of frontier defence.

On the 1st January 1892, Sir Frederick was raised to the peerage, as Baron Roberts of Kandahar and Waterford, and a year later he left India, after forty-one years' service, for good.

On his return from Afghanistan he had been called the "most popular man in England"; now he might be termed, on his departure from his command, the most popular man in the army. "Bobs" was essentially the soldiers' general, and all ranks, British and Native alike, looked on the general with genuine feelings of love and admiration.

Two years after his return to England, he was promoted to be Field-Marshal.

It was during his term of service as Commander-in-Chief of the Forces in Ireland, that Lord Roberts was again called upon to lead his country's armies.

The fatal peace of Majuba Hill—"a peace which was no peace"—was about to reap a harvest of disaster and bloodshed.

In the autumn of 1899, the Transvaal Republic, joined

by the Orange Free State, declared war on Great Britain. They had been preparing for war for a long time, and in a short time the British colonies in South Africa were invaded by a well-equipped, hostile force.

Then came bad news fast—the fight at Talana Hill, the retirement on Ladysmith, the battles of Belmont, Graspan, and Modder River. These were the dark days of the war.

People at home, as the newsboys in the murky November afternoons shouted their tale of fresh disaster, caught their breath, and wondered if this was the beginning of the end—if the sun of British power was about to set.

The feeling everywhere grew that there was one man who could save the Empire, and turn defeat into victory. All eyes were turned towards "Roberts, the deliverer," as he was already felt to be. At length the Government asked him to take the chief command in South Africa.

"My Lord, for nineteen years I have led an abstemious life in the hope of this day," came the reply.

During the preceding week the worst news that had reached England for a century came pouring in. Buller had moved to cross the Tugela, but under the terrible fire of the Boers had been forced to retire, and Ladysmith, with its heroic garrison, was still unrelieved.

During this fight Lord Roberts' only son had been mortally wounded, and had died the following day. Like his father, years before, at Delhi, he had been shot down whilst gallantly saving the guns. As in the case of the father, a V.C. was assigned to him; but alas! it was only to his parents that the honour could be sent.

In spite of personal grief, in spite of the weight of years, Lord Roberts was ready at the nation's call. Nor did he long delay: a week was all the time he asked for, in which to make his preparations. Two days before Christmas he sailed from Southampton, carrying with him the hopes and anxious wishes of a mighty Empire.

"Three English forces were apparently helpless in the face of the armed positions occupied by the Boers; three towns on English soil were beleaguered by hostile forces; three great reverses had befallen three English generals; and 11,000 of the best troops of this country were entangled in Ladysmith. On Saturday, the 16th, we sent for Lord Roberts, and on the following Saturday he was on the high seas."

In these brief words did Mr. Arthur Balfour afterwards sum up the position of affairs, and pay a tribute to the dauntless soldier.

Meanwhile, on board the *Balmoral Castle*, the active brain of the general was busy, and when, on the 10th of January, the ship reached Capetown, Lord Roberts was ready with his plan of campaign.

No longer was Cronje's taunt, that the British were "tied by the leg to the railway," to hold good. The little man, who had marched from Kabul to Kandahar, had his method of attack prepared, and was ready to move swiftly and strike hard.

Some time had, however, to be spent at Capetown

before all the arrangements could be made. Finally, on the 6th of February, Lord Roberts left Capetown, and two days after he reached the Modder River camp. Here for two or three days he remained, his head-quarters for the time being the railway carriage in which he had travelled.

"Ladysmith must be relieved," Lord Roberts had from the first declared.

On the 15th the relief of Kimberley was accomplished, and this success roused the spirits of all—the soldiers fighting in the field, and the anxious watchers at home. Back from Kimberley French and his tired cavalry rode: the great object now was to round up Cronje and his army.

At Paardeberg, Cronje and his Boers lay, lulled by a feeling of false security. Gradually the British forces under Lord Roberts drew the net closer.

The Boer general was taken by surprise; in spite of repeated warnings, he had scoffed at the idea of a British army moving so swiftly and so secretly. Little did he know the man he had to do with, this new general who had infused such life and activity into his troops.

The Boer leader at last saw that his position was getting desperate; already he could be seen signalling frantically for help. At sunrise, on the 18th February, he woke to find himself "hopelessly and helplessly beleaguered." "'Bobs' had got old Cronje at last," the soldiers said.

On the 27th day of February, the anniversary of the Boer victory at Majuba Hill, the end came. The white flag went up, and Cronje and his burghers, to the number of about four thousand men, laid down their arms.

For nineteen long years the Boers had taunted the Englishmen and boasted of their victory, saying how, if ever war again broke out, they would drive the red-coats to the sea. Now, at last, the day of reckoning had come, and they themselves were to know the bitterness of defeat.

The very day Cronje surrendered, General Buller, after desperate fighting, found the way to Ladysmith practically open; and, on the 3rd of March, his army was able to join hands with the gallant garrison.

Success followed success; ever moving onwards, the army reached Bloemfontein, the capital of the Orange Free State. The town surrendered promptly, and Lord Roberts hoisted the British flag, a silk Union Jack, worked especially for the occasion by Lady Roberts' own hands.

Here the army rested for a bit, but soon they were on the march again, and closing in on Johannesburg—"the golden city"—which surrendered on the 31st of May, and was occupied by our troops. Again the army pressed on, this time to Pretoria, and Roberts, playing for a great stake, launched his troops at the Boers, and again was victorious, and the capital of the Transvaal was in the hands of the British.

The fighting still went on, however, round the city, and it was not till seven days afterwards that the Boers were finally dispersed, and driven from the neighbourhood of Pretoria.

At Bergendal, Buller and the men from Natal again defeated the Boers, and this was the last great fight of the war.

How long the Boers still in the field resisted we all know, but the backbone of the fighting had been broken, and Lord Roberts' work was done. He had marched and fought his forces over a huge area—an area greater than France, Germany, and Austria. The war was now practically over: the veteran fighter had turned gloom into joy, defeat into victory. His work was done, and the time had come for him to say farewell to the gallant army he had so ably led.

The lessons of the war still remain. It has knit together the whole British Empire. It was a war fought not alone by a British army, but by the militia, yeomanry, and volunteers of Great Britain, and by our brothers across the sea—the men of South Africa, Canada, Australia, New Zealand, India, and Ceylon. Lord Roberts was the first general to command an army of Britain and of Greater Britain—an imperial host.

The mother country had been in sore distress, and her children in the colonies had heard the parent voice and hastened to her aid.

"So we stand," said Lord Roberts, in his farewell address at Capetown, "and please God, will continue to stand, a united, world-wide dominion, bound together by indissoluble ties, and ever ready to carry out the destiny of our race. God has brought us out of what in the dark days of last December appeared to be the valley of the shadow of death, and we can now look back on those days of tribulation with deep gratitude for the mercy vouchsafed to the Queen's troops."

On the 2nd of January Igor, Lord Roberts reached England, and next day he rendered his last obeisance to the Queen he had served so long and so faithfully. From her dying hands almost he received, as reward for his latest and greatest services, the Order of the Knight of the Garter and an Earldom. A few days later he entered on his new duties as Commander-in-Chief, and at this post he remained for three years.

The veteran Field-Marshal had more than doubled the span allotted. by the ancient law of India, which says that a man shall be twenty years a fighter. But, though he had reached the verge of threescore and ten years, the rest he had earned had no attractions for him as long as there was work to be done. "The truth is," he had said, "that the mother country takes long to understand that the best way to avoid war is to be well prepared for it."

He who was ever ready to take the field at a moment's notice, in order to fight the enemies of his country, now set himself the task of preparing the country itself for the stern duties of war.

"I shall continue to work for the army as long as I can work at all," Lord Roberts has said. "The experience I have gained will greatly help me in the work that lies before me, which is, I conceive, to make the army of the United

Kingdom as perfect as it is possible for any army to be. *This I shall strive to do with all my might.*"

But it is not only with the regular army that Lord Roberts is concerned.

On every occasion has he urged the youth of our country to train themselves to arms, as the only real means of peace and of safeguarding our Empire.

Under his fostering care a spirit of patriotism has been awakened, and it is to be hoped that the day is not far distant when every able-bodied man in the country will have learnt to be able to shoot, and to fight, if necessary, for his hearth and home. Then—

"Come the four corners of the world in arms, And we shall shock them: nought shall make us rue, If England to itself do rest but true."

"Ok, but I'll be watching you." He smiled and gave a million-dollar wink.

"Diablo, girl, if only your cousin wasn't gay! I'd be all over that." Nikki gave me her dazzling smile as he herded us past the line at the ID check and cashier.

"Follow me." Angel grabbed my hand and guiding me past the crowds to a table near the bar that read, Reserved. "You ladies hang out here; I'll be back in a bit. Pero cuidate, ok?"

"Claro!"

I took a second to soak it all in. We were in an expansive Caribbean-style room with vaulted and exposed white wooden trusses, white columns, and tropical plants lining the background. The club wasn't packed yet, but I could tell from the vibe that a truly lively party was about to go down. As we stood by our VIP table, three different guys tried to hit on us and were quickly dismissed. As many others followed our every movement with their eyes.

Angel returned just a few minutes later with two cocktails. "Here you go, ladies. It's good to know people, right?"

Just then, a leggy blonde came and told him something we couldn't interpret, and he was off again.

"Salud," we both said at the same time.

Feeling the positive vibes, we danced to the pulsing sounds of dance-hall music. We drank and laughed and flirted until Nikki nudged me with her elbow.

"Hey girl, look over there, at the DJ booth. One for you, one for me." She had her arm curled around mine and I followed her eyes with mine.

Chapter Four

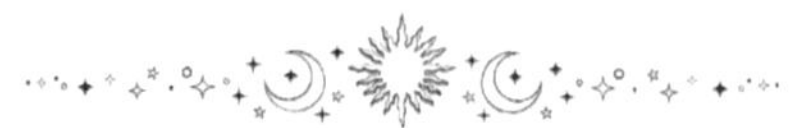

"Oh no, Nikki. Listen, I'm not trying to hook up with anyone, ok? I've got to focus on school. That's all I'm about right now." I was annoyed she was even asking. I rolled my eyes.

Nikki grabbed my arm and pulled me to the DJ booth. She found a space for us to dance with a direct line of sight to the two DJs. She started staring and smiling at one of them, and he waved her over. I stayed right where I was.

A few minutes later, she returned, and slid her hand around my arm. "Ok, so they're asking us to come join them at their booth. Just come along, ok? They won't bite." She had to tug at my arm to get me to move, and I trudged up the steps behind her.

"Hey, I'm Shawn, and that's my boy, Omar." Shawn pointed to the other DJ working the turntables.

Omar dripped with rhythm. His beige, long-sleeve pullover hugged his muscular build and so did his jeans that tapered at the bottom. He had creamy, honey-colored skin, and he wore a short beard that suited his sharp jawline. Apparently, Nikki had quickly gotten acquainted with Shawn, because when he sat on the couch, she went and sat right on his lap.

I rolled my eyes again. There was a bottle on the table, and a waitress came over and served us each a drink. I took it down in one shot. My feet felt restless just standing there doing nothing, as the beats resounded in my ears, so I got up and started dancing.

I guess I had a little too much, because I didn't realize it when Shawn went back to the booth and Omar stood behind me, moving to the merengue beat. He was exactly the kind of boy I needed to stay away from, but a little merengue wouldn't hurt. His full lips worked up into a smile when I turned around and moved my hips to his rhythm. I bit down on my lip when he placed his hand at my side and twirled me around on the beat.

Twenty minutes later, we were still at it, and I had to stop before I worked up a sweat and messed up my hair.

"Let me get your number before I have to go back in the DJ booth." He held out his phone.

I grabbed it from his hand and took a selfie, then texted it to myself. "There, now you have my number, and tomorrow you'll remember who I was."

He chuckled and slid the phone back in his pocket.

I hadn't realized a crowd had formed around us, a tangle of bodies pulsing to the Latin beats. As soon as I stopped dancing, a few people were quick to take up my dance space, inching closer to me, and I inched closer to Omar. I placed a hand on his solid, defined chest and the other at his side, then looked up into his almond-shaped eyes. My cheeks flushed as I got closer to him and I knew right then he would be big trouble.

He returned my stare and I could feel the warmth of our connection charge through my hands and into my skin. My eyes moved down and lingered on his lips. I craved them on mine, but I had just met the guy. It would have to wait until I knew him a little better. I pulled back from him, and before I could remove my hands from his body, he pulled me in a little closer and bent his head a tiny bit more. Subtle and smooth.

His lips were inches from mine when I felt a tug on my shoulder and saw a tattooed arm shove him back. Omar's eyes narrowed, and his jaw clenched something fierce. The crowd sensed the energy shift and stepped back from us.

"Back off, Omar. She's not one of your hoes." Elio stood there at eye level with Omar, and I couldn't remember when I had seen him this pissed.

I wasn't his property. I could do what I wanted.

"What is your deal?" I yelled at Elio.

"You better step the fuck off," Omar growled, and his hands curled into fists at his side.

Elio glared at him.

"There's plenty of other women." Elio opened his arms wide and gestured to where a group of hot ladies stood watching to see how this all went down.

Omar stepped up and met Elio eye to eye.

Then I felt a tug at my arm. Nikki pulled me back from the center. "I heard Elio talking when you guys were dancing," she whispered in my ear while not taking her eyes off the two of them standing on the dance floor. "Omar is in the Sangre Cartel. When Elio saw you dancing with Omar, he went ballistic."

They looked like they were about to pound each other over me, and even though I was an Aries and loved all the attention, I couldn't let them do it.

I snatched my arm from Nikki's grasp and stepped between them. "Elio, you're not my dad. I can dance with whoever I want."

"Sasha, this is between me and him." He glared at me.

Omar nodded to Shawn who stood to the right of me. He grabbed me and pulled me back. His grip was much tighter than Nikki's and even though I struggled, I couldn't break free. The second he pulled me back Omar swung without hesitation, and the first blow landed right across Elio's temple, catching him by surprise.

He stumbled quickly, then straightened out. Elio rushed at Omar and tried to return the favor with a haymaker that took Omar off balance while he tried to knock his head off. Omar's eyes locked on Elio when he took another swing, and Elio ducked just in time to miss it. Elio's expression darkened as he dealt a serious blow to Omar's jaw. Omar fell back with a scowl, and he grimaced as Elio pushed into him with a few more blows.

The crowd cheered and gasped at the fight as the two of them went at it. Elio slammed Omar into the DJ booth, and Omar gasped for breath. Elio didn't waste any time and pounced on him while he was down, but Omar kicked out with his right leg and shoved Elio back into the turntables. As the records screeched, all of the clubbers on the main dance floor turned to watch the commotion in the DJ booth.

"Let me go!" I yelled at Shawn as I fought against him.

"You know that mafia king, don't you? Omar isn't going to like that," he growled.

"Look, I'm not mafia, ok? I don't have anything to do with this. You can let me go," I insisted, but he ignored me.

Omar's veins pulsed with intensity, and I could see his eyes start to turn red with rage. He focused in and took another swing that rocked across Elio's face. Elio bounced right back and went in fast with two more blows at Omar, but only landed one. Elio's face scrunched up with anger as he shoved his body weight into Omar again, knocking him into a group of girls standing by a high bar. He took a quick jab at his face and broke the skin above Omar's eye. Blood dripped from his eyebrow onto his cheek and stained his shirt. That only seemed to make Omar angrier as he shoved Elio back and landed several right hooks into his side.

The music stopped, and the lights turned on. Everyone was staring at the two fighting in the VIP area when the sound of gunshots rang out inside the club. People started to panic and run in all directions. Shawn finally let me go, and I looked around for Nikki. She was making her way to me through the crowd that pushed up and around her. She grabbed my hand, and I looked around for Elio and Omar, but they had stopped fighting and disappeared into the crowd somewhere.

"Let's get the hell out," I told Nikki.

We were both shaken up from the fight as we drove home. "So, Omar and Elio hate each other? Did you know this?" I asked Nikki.

"Not until tonight. Girl, you know how to pick 'em." She grinned.

"I told you I didn't even want to talk to them. Did you know he was a Sangre? That's a huge red flag." I wasn't in the mafia, but I grew up with Elio and his crew. Obviously, I would be loyal to them.

"I just met them tonight, just like you!" she insisted.

As I was just getting home I got a text from Elio: *You ok?*

Yeah. I'm fine, I wrote back. *You?*

Yeah, all good.

I stared at my phone for a few seconds, expecting him to write something. I was still upset at him for feeling the need to fight Omar just because I had danced with him. I didn't belong to anyone.

I'm waiting for my apology. We'd known each other so long, I could forgive him for that as long as he apologized.

And I'm waiting for mine.

What?! No way. I didn't know he was Sangre.

In that case, I forgive you.

Was he serious?

Great, I texted back. *Now where's mine?*

He ghosted me after that.

Chapter Five

My father struggled daily with his demons. If he would brush his black hair—and shave—he could be a handsome man of six foot two with a strong build. My mother swears he was different before he was outcasted by the mafia for snitching once when he was arrested, even though he swears he never did. Rumor has it the only reason they let him live was because no one could ever prove he actually did snitch. It was just a theory. It could have been anyone that gave them up to the Miami police, but it didn't matter. After that, no one ever trusted him again.

I have a few memories from when I was little of spending hours with him at his shop. I loved watching him put together and pull apart everything mechanical. Whenever I watched him, I imagined he could hear the mechanical pieces speak to him. It was as though they would bend to his will and do whatever he wanted. As I got older, he would give me my own projects to work on, and that's when I discovered I had a real knack for it. We were both Aries signs, and my Titi Lily once told me that he and I would have a lot in common.

But I had nothing in common with him. He'd always drank, but his drinking had gotten worse after that night when he'd come home bloodied and beat up like I had never seen him.

My parents never talked about what happened that night, but I figured he tried to get back in with the mafia and it all went sideways. I heard from Elio that one of the bosses was giving him a second chance but he was too drunk to get the safe open. Ever since then, it's like he just gave up on himself.

After his daily visit to the liquor store, he'd return with a bottle wrapped in crisp brown paper, the magic potion—rather, poison—that numbed the pain of his past and the burdens of the future. I guessed it helped him dump his empty, depressing memories into the deep recesses of his mind. This also meant any time I tried to connect with him, I would be disappointed.

Now I just never tried.

Where there was once affection, our relationship dissipated into tolerance, and later, into resentment. But my mother Lola still held on. She depended on his approval. He was the man she would never give up on and gave everything up for. It was a slippery slope to invest in someone who didn't have anything to give.

A few days had passed since the incident at the club. I was just getting home from class and went to the kitchen for a snack, and afterward, I planned to get to my schoolwork. It was dim in the cluttered kitchen. There were dishes with old food piled around the sink and not much to eat in the refrigerator. Unlike Nikki's house, ours was falling apart, with water stains on the ceiling and cabinet doors that fell off their hinges. The house wasn't necessarily messy, but it was unloved. We had the added bonus of living in one of the worst neighborhoods downtown. The night brought the constant sirens of police cars, with neighbors either partying or yelling at each other and the occasional gunshot ringing out.

I settled on eating a peanut-butter-and-jelly sandwich. As I laid out the bread and smeared the creamy peanut butter on a fluffy white slice, Dante strolled into the kitchen. Reeking of rum and Coke, he sported a white wifebeater with blue jeans. Such a stereotype.

His dull, glossy eyes caught mine, and when I looked into them, I couldn't look away. There was a dark pull in those eyes; images of death and loneliness echoed in my mind. I snapped out of it when he snarled at me. The tattoos that lined a muscular chest and forearms—thanks to regular bench presses with the weight set he kept in the backyard—looked particularly sinister. I heard mumblings that the tattoos represented the people he'd killed in mafia wars before he had us kids and broke away from that life. I didn't know for sure, and wasn't sure I ever wanted to know.

Dante approached the bottle of dark rum on the counter, pouring it gently over ice. Delicately, he replaced the cap and set the bottle back down. With his glass now poured, he turned to me and slurred, "Who just dropped you off, and where were you this afternoon?"

He never asked me anything. Not about school, not about work and not about my favorite flavor of ice cream.

"What do you care?" I replied, instantly regretting the short answer.

His forehead wrinkled as he looked down at his hand, and we both watched as he slowly curled each finger, one by one, into a fist. Clenched tight, the fist moved into a fully packed right hook that landed with precision on my left cheekbone.

My dear father, no longer boxing in the ring, slammed into me so hard I flew across the room.

Thrust backward, I banged my back on the kitchen counter and bounced right off, falling to the floor. This wasn't the first time he'd hit me, but still, every time it was a surprise. I curled into a ball on the dirty tiles. I sobbed quietly with not so much as a glance in his direction so he wouldn't call me weak.

Dante paused for a second to contemplate me like a hunter would an injured deer. He grabbed his cup with ice and rum and walked away. I wasn't sure where he went afterward; I was very sure I didn't care.

We went without speaking for what felt like weeks after that. He never apologized, but Lola told me I had to. She always apologized to him after *he* beat *her*. When I was twelve, we left in the middle of the night after he'd almost strangled her to death. The three of us slept in the car because she had nowhere to go. She went back to him the very next day, and he was still sleeping when we got home. He hadn't even noticed we'd left.

I would be different, I told myself. I would learn how to defend myself physically, and if I couldn't, then at least I would emotionally. I wouldn't build that emotional wall the social media therapists always warned us about. Those were penetrable. Walls could be demolished. Instead, I would fly.

⸺ ⟡ ⸺

My feet were already off the ground, and my hands were in front of me where I could see them. I was soaring. My home was just underneath me and got smaller as I soared higher and higher. Where should I go? I wanted to relax, to feel safe, but there was no safe place. I decided I would just keep flying until I saw something that felt right.

I began to leave the city. Rooftops became scarce and I saw the woods farther out behind my house. My body was being pulled down. I began descending but didn't want to . . . What was happening? There was a patch of land; I could see the ground now. My feet touched down, and I heard the crunch of leaves and twigs underneath my sneakers. Trees surrounded me, with vines and bushes that blocked my ability to see far. Yet there was a formless movement about fifty feet away.

I shuddered when I saw that familiar black-and-gray mist fast approaching. This damn thing was on repeat in my nightmares. It moved like smoke or haze, and whenever it came close, it would scare the shit out of me. It was like every single one of my fears came to life inside of it and it just wanted to suck me in. Yet, there was still a part of me that wanted to let it.

Closer now, I demanded, "Who are you? What do you want?"

The Shadow let out an answer from its depth with the sound the sound of thousand whispering voices and an ominous tone. It wasn't like it came from one person. Instead, the voice seemed to surround me and fill me with a state of knowing. "I am your shadow. You can try to fly, but I will always catch you."

The vibration of these words brushed against my very flesh, as if the sound itself was composed of physical matter, of souls and spirits and inexplicable shadow beasts spanning centuries.

My heart pounded as the Shadow hovered and started to envelop me. It covered every inch of my flesh, and I felt electric charges all over my skin. As vibrations of doom covered me, I began to have a vision of fire. A fire that surrounded me completely. I became that very image as flames licked and flickered up my hands and arms until I was entirely covered in a blaze of crimson and gold. Although I could feel heat surround me, my flesh didn't burn. I didn't feel the pain of it. I only saw myself within these flames.

More afraid than confused at what was happening to me, I remembered I could fly, and I shot myself up fiercely into the darkened sky. The wind that whipped around me smothered out the fire. The last thing to strip away was the shadow-mist that had started it all, and it seemed to group together underneath me. The shadow of doom continued to follow me as I flew. It stayed beneath me until I reached my home once again. I entered my room, and chills riddled my body to wake.

CHAPTER SIX

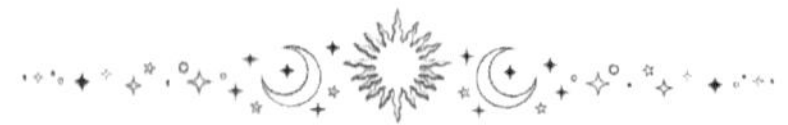

A few more weeks had gone by since the incident at the club and Elio still hadn't texted me. Today my horoscope said I would be easily distracted, and it couldn't have been more accurate.

I was on my bed, lying on my stomach, about to open a textbook laid out in front of me. *Ding.* My phone showed that a text had come in from Nikki. I propped myself up on my elbows to read it.

Hey girl, what are you up to? Did you hear about the party Saturday? She was talking about Elio's older brother's party. Everyone in his gang would most likely be there.

I can't, I replied. *I have finals on Monday. #focus #goals.*

Damn, why are you always studying?

I told you, I need to graduate.

Somehow, I'd managed to pass all my classes. I wasn't giving up now.

Just then, my phone rang, and the caller ID said Omar. I knew I should just ignore him and forget about that night, but another part of me was still pissed at Elio for thinking he could control me. He couldn't tell me who I could or couldn't date. I'd thought about it a lot since that night, and even though I hadn't called Omar myself, I knew I would answer the phone if he called me. The mafia had never exactly been good to us. My father was a ruined man because of them, and I seemed to be following in his footsteps. Maybe Omar was the fresh start I needed.

"Hey," I responded, surprised to be hearing from him at all after all that went down.

"What are you doin'?" His voice was steady and polite.

"Studying. I have a test tomorrow." Even though I hadn't studied at all. I really didn't know why he was calling me now that he knew I had was a friend of his enemy gang.

"All right."

"Ok, so that's it?" I hoped he noticed the flat tone of my voice.

"What do you mean, *that's it*?" He'd definitely noticed.

Right then, I wanted to ask him why he was calling now, after weeks had gone by since the fight. I wanted to know how he expected us to be friends after all that had gone down in the club. I mean, how could this whole thing between him and me even work, and why would he bother when he could have so many other girls? I wanted to tell him not to call me again because I was focused on studying and he was a major problem. So, I just wanted him to get to it. What did he want?

But my problem, once again, was that I didn't say any of this. I remembered his combination of honey-colored skin, tall, muscular physique, and sharp jawline that made him just so fine. On top of that, everyone knew that the Sangre Cartel pulled in a whole lot of money, and the fact that he was calling me at all meant he was still interested. For whatever reason, all these thoughts kept me from saying what I should have.

"I mean, is there something on your mind? Something you want to talk about?" I worked on covering up all the thoughts swimming in my head.

"Just wanted to see if we could hang out."

"You know, after everything that happened the other night, I don't think that's a good idea. I don't want to look over my shoulder every time I'm out with you." I mean, he was almost worth the risk, but up until this point in my life, the only two people I could ever count on were Elio and Nikki. I couldn't go behind Elio's back now, or could I?

"That's too bad. Call me back if you change your mind."

He needed to know where my loyalty lay. He was just asking for trouble.

"Yeah. I guess. I better get back to studying."

What was he playing at? Did he like me that much, or was this some kind of territory war that I'd started? And I don't know, but maybe part of me liked the attention. Either way, his phone call meant I was on his mind and he was willing to risk another fight to hang out with me.

I threw myself back on my bed and looked up at the ceiling with wide-open arms. I closed my eyes and pictured him.

It was in this stillness that I saw a little shadow, like a black cat scurrying by, and I considered the possibility that this was all a game to him. He gets in a fight in the club over me, and he doesn't call until two months later. Two whole months. Elio would be so pissed if he knew I'd even answered the phone. I owed a lot to Elio. So many times I'd needed some extra money for school lunch, all those times his family had invited me over for Thanksgiving and Christmas dinners that my family had somehow forgotten to have. I opened my eyes and looked at the ceiling. No, I could never turn my back on Elio.

I picked up my phone to send Omar one final text: *Delete my number*.

And I deleted his.

Chapter Seven

We were at Nikki's house getting dressed for the party. I tugged a tight-fitting white tube top over my head, then pulled up loose, high-waisted jeans and completed the ensemble with a thin cheetah-print belt and brown cork wedges. Nikki was wearing a black tank top, beige linen overall shorts and strappy sandals.

While we put on makeup and finished our hair Nikki turned to me. "I meant to tell you before. You know Anthony that works at Monty's? Well, he said he saw your mom there, grinding with some guy on the dance floor."

"Here, try this gloss over that color. It'll work great with your skin," I told her enthusiastically, ignoring her comment about my mom.

She took the gloss and tried it out. "You're right, it looks nice."

"It looks perfect! You can have it." I slipped my purse over my shoulder and stood by the door.

"What about your mom?" she asked.

"What about her? No big deal. She told me all about her girls' night out, ok? Tony is just trying to stir things up—you know how he is."

We pulled up to a middle-class home in a more-than-decent neighborhood. There were already several cars in the driveway, and dancehall music spilled out onto the street. As we entered the cookie-cutter suburban home, I saw several people milling about, but the place was far from packed. On the plush gray couch sat some teenagers; a few young-adult men chatted loudly in the kitchen. Caribbean music played in the background.

We found a place to sit under the fan on the patio, then we easily integrated with a few other people we'd just met. Not too much time had passed before Elio appeared with his arm around a gorgeous woman about my age with high cheekbones, straight black hair, delicately slanted eyelids and creamy, Jamaican-caramel skin. Was this his girlfriend? Stars, she was gorgeous. I couldn't help but gawk at them, and wondered if he could tell I was trying to figure them out.

Elio had a wide, alluring smile as he laughed casually with the woman. His dark beard was freshly groomed, and his thick black hair combed but loose. He didn't seem to even notice the evil eye I was giving him.

She was probably a good friend, I told myself; it was no big deal. He was just flirting.

After whispering in the woman's ear, Elio looked over at me and stepped away from the beauty. He came to us and shooed away the Rasta teenager sitting next to me and made himself comfortable. As he did, he put his hand on my leg as if he had every right. Irritated, I looked at his hand, then his face.

I had to satisfy my curiosity. "Who's she?" I asked intensely.

"Who? That girl over there? That's Lynn. She's just a friend. A business partner." He was playing it down.

"What kind of business partner?"

"The kind that makes lots of money for both of us. Now, let me hit that spliff." He brushed me off.

As he turned to talk to the Rasta, Nikki looked at me with both eyebrows raised. The idea that that woman could be that gorgeous and be respected by Elio as a business partner just made my blood boil. I felt an unnatural heat rise to my hands and lifted them up from my thighs to cool them down. What was up with my hands heating up like this every time I got mad?

"Did you hear that?" Nikki whispered to me. "He said, 'The kind that makes lots of money.' I wonder what she does."

"Yes, girl, I heard," I answered with my eyes focused on my red hands. Maybe they'd laced the weed and it was starting to get to my head. I couldn't let Elio think his little show with the new girl had fazed me. Anyway, why would it? Elio was like a brother to me.

A few hours passed, Nikki had disappeared, and I was talking about a new album with some of the people I'd just met. "Every song is lit. Every single song," I was saying when Nikki came up and interrupted me.

"Hey, come over here." Her eyes narrowed on me.

"Yo, where've you been?" I put my arm around her waist.

She pushed it aside and looked at me seriously. "So, you know how we're always complaining about money? I'm so over it. Plus, I read my horoscope today, and it said that a business opportunity was going to come out of the blue from my social circles. This is it. I can feel it." Her face was bright and excited.

"Yeah, but what else did it say?" My head tilted to one side, and my lips flattened into a thin line.

"Fine, it also said to tread lightly, because all that shines isn't gold," she mumbled, not meeting my eye.

She was right about our financial situation. We were always running some scam to get cash. Just yesterday we were at a gas station telling a story to a nice old man about how we needed gas money to get home, when all we really wanted it for was to help pay my tuition. He went to pay the attendant for the gas instead of giving us the twenty dollars, and as soon as he began to pump, the tank overflowed.

"The mafia has a job coming up, and it sounds to me like they need someone like you." She smiled from ear to ear. "This is our chance to prove ourselves, Sasha. You can get out from under Elio's shadow and show them your skills."

CHAPTER EIGHT

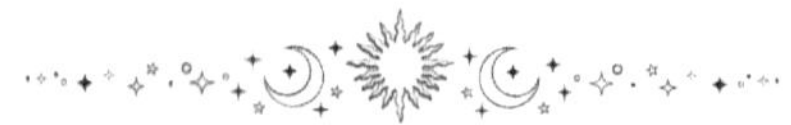

I leaned in closer to her on the couch. "Tell me everything."

"Well, turns out that girl Elio was with works for this guy named Razor, he's one of the heads of the mafia. He's in the next room playing cards." Her eyes shifted to a door by the main room. She went on, "She's been dating one of the biggest commercial real estate developers in Miami. The guy built almost all the luxury high rises downtown. Looks like they've been watching him for a while and now they're ready to make a move on one of his locations." Her voice was hushed as she leaned in further. "They said they need someone that can do what you do." I recognized the look that said a plan was forming.

"How do you know all this?"

"Well"—the side of her mouth turned up slightly—"I was making out with Pablo on the couch while they were talking and heard everything. It's called multitasking."

We both laughed.

"Yep," she continued. "I told Pablo you could do the job. He said no at first, but then I told him how good you were." She grabbed my hand, and we began walking. "And I gave him some extra attention to help him think about it." She gave me a wink.

We walked into what looked like a wolves' den with the number of men sprawled around the room. As soon as we passed over the threshold, the smell of alcohol and smoke surrounded us. Two men sat at a small table playing cards.

Nikki walked me closer to them, and as we stood off to the side they kept playing as if we weren't there.

Nikki whispered in my ear, "That's Pablo's uncle. They call him Razor. No one knows his real name."

As she was whispering, Razor looked at Nikki and said, "Pablo tells me you want to work for us now, do you?"

Nikki answered, "Well, my girl Sasha here, she's who you need. There's no one better."

He stared us both up and down and turned back to the cards. I wanted to trace my fingers along the scar that went down his dark cheek.

He played the ace of spades and won the hand, then he turned to look at Nikki again. "You know how to play Spades?"

"Of course!" Nikki slinked into her chair.

I moved more slowly and worked to keep my chin high as I sat down. He dealt us both in, and we joined him in the hand. After a few rounds, I was winning, and Razor finally took a second to look at me. This was the first time he'd set his eyes on me since I'd entered the room.

"You don't look like much to me. I don't think you're ready," he deadpanned.

"You're right—she's not ready," a voice said from the doorway.

I turned my head and saw Elio standing there, his gaze dark and direct, with one of his boys next to him. Now, I respected Elio, but I was over him not giving me a chance. He never brought me in on the bigger deals like these, and I was missing out on making a lot of money. Plus, now he was interfering with my love life and it was a complete double standard.

"Elio, good to see you, man." Razor lifted his gaze to meet Elio's and cracked a smile I thought couldn't exist on his face.

"I get to say when I'm ready, and I am definitely ready now." I didn't want anyone speaking for me, ever.

"Come here, Sasha. Let me talk to you a minute," Elio commanded and walked out of the room.

My eyes met Razor's, and I tried to read him. Whose word was he going to take? From his blank expression, it seemed like I needed Elio's blessing. I stood and walked out of the room after Elio.

"Is this about your father? Is he at it again? I swear, if he hurt you..." His eyes felt like they were piercing into my soul.

"No. I mean, yes," I stuttered, doing my best to hide the thunderstorm of nerves in my chest. I shook my head. Many times, he'd sat and wiped my tears after tough days with my father at home. "I can do this." My tone was much calmer than I expected. "I need the job, Elio. You know I've got to get out of that house."

His eyes flashed with anger, then reason seemed to wash over him. "This is much bigger than anything you've done for me. If you mess this up, I won't be able to cover for you." His eyebrows pinched at the thought and his face darkened.

"I know, but if not now, Elio, when? You know I can do this. When have I ever messed up?" I tightened my jaw.

"Fine."

It took me a moment for that to sink in. I uncrossed my arms and reached over to kiss him on the cheek. My hands rested lightly on his chest, and I felt that familiar warmth come from him.

He turned his head toward mine, and the corners of his eyes gave away his concern. "But you let me negotiate the terms. I don't want them thinking they can take advantage of you because you're new. And I'm part of the deal. You don't do it alone. If anyone tries to talk to you or get you to do anything you don't want to do, you let me know. Right away, ok?"

"Deal." I had to work to contain my excitement.

Elio did just as he'd promised and handled the negotiation. I would be paid fifteen hundred dollars for opening the safe at the developer's site. The safe was where the developer kept all the petty cash used to pay workers under the table, and for supplies that needed to be handled as cash transactions. On a normal day, the amount they stored in there wasn't worth the risk to the mafia. But Lynn had learned that they would be holding twenty-five thousand dollars there next week as an incentive to pay a small-time local politician to speed up the permitting process.

Once Elio had convinced Razor I was the right person for the job, Razor turned to me and said, "I'm only giving you this chance because of Elio. I trust him... Now, what do you need?"

"I need to find out everything about the safe." I focused on Razor and stared intently into his deep, black eyes. "The make, the model, the serial number. The size. The color. I want every detail. I'll need pictures and video. Have her zoom in on the keypad, the keyhole, the dial. Everything."

"You sound like your father," Razor slurred.

I flinched. I thought he was long forgotten by the mafia. But now that I thought about it, Razor looked like he could be just a few years younger than Dante. It shouldn't surprise me that they knew each other.

"I'm not like my father." My lips tightened.

"I'll take Elio's word for it. If anything happens on the job site, it's his ass," Razor hissed.

I knew then that Elio had put himself on the line for me.

Razor slapped down the king of spades on top of my jack. "Lynn, come over here," he yelled.

She stood up from the other side of the room and walked over. Her eyes were dead set on me.

"Show her the pictures."

She reached into the back pocket of her tight jeans and flipped through her phone to find the pictures, then handed her phone to me.

I swiped through about thirty photos and videos of exactly what I needed. "Great, I can work with this."

Chapter Nine

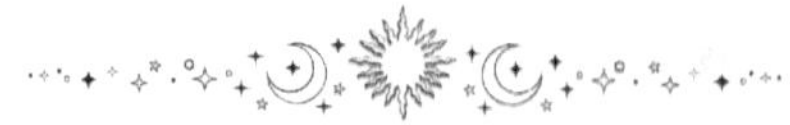

While I was waiting for Elio to take me over to Razor's, I reviewed my tools for the fifth time since that morning. My stomach felt like I'd swallowed a bag of tiny needles, and they were poking from all directions. I pressed on, packing the tools carefully and bringing double just in case I dropped something. Elio picked me up, and we drove to Razor's house together. Moments like these I really missed Nikki. She had a way of putting me at ease like no one else. She had been trying to convince me all week that she should come and carry my tools, but I finally talked her out of it. If we got caught, I didn't want her to go down for just carrying a bag of tools.

Elio and I didn't talk much in the car on the way there. He seemed tense as he gripped the steering wheel.

"Are we ok?" I asked.

He looked over at me, slow and controlled. "Yeah. All good." He turned the radio up.

I stared out the window at the full moon overhead and was reassured after reading my horoscope for the day, which said: *Friday's Scorpio moon encourages you to engage in whatever's waiting to be unearthed. Uranus may bring unfamiliar territory to your finances and work projects. This might throw you into a panic, but don't fall into this trap. Aim to remain focused and keep your thoughts to yourself.*

We arrived at Razor's house, and he appeared in the hallway.

"Come with me." He turned back around and walked into the kitchen. He was all business. "Lynn confirmed they dropped off the bag this afternoon. She's with him on his yacht now and won't be back until tomorrow. This is our window. I'll take care of security, and Elio will drive." Razor turned to me. "You know what your job is."

I nodded; it was simple enough. "What are we doing about the cameras?"

"It's all taken care of." Razor narrowed his eyes just a bit. "We will be wearing these hats." He handed me a black baseball cap with what appeared to be a computer chip displayed on the bill. "This chip emits infrared light that can't be picked up by cameras. We'll be invisible."

I wanted to believe him, but it sounded crazy.

"Don't worry, we tested it out with their cameras the other day." Razor shrugged casually. "Lynn flirted with the security guard while she looked over his shoulder, and all he saw were blasts of white light where people were standing. They work. Trust me."

I would have to trust him, then. He explained that the infrared diffraction chips worked better than taking out all the cameras one by one because there could be hidden cameras around. I took a deep breath when I remembered my horoscope and thought, *This is what it meant by don't panic.*

We traveled in a black minivan and pulled up to a parking lot down the street from the construction site. The safe was inside the mobile office unit, which was surrounded by a metal gate. A security detail stood just outside. The whole thing should take no longer than five minutes.

I felt those needles poking in my belly again as I watched Razor get out of the car and approach the security guard, who was watching something on his phone. He didn't even notice when Razor went right up to him and knocked the side of his head with his fist. The guard slumped to the ground, and Razor quickly pulled his body inside the gate where we couldn't see him.

Elio got a text. He looked up at me and said, "Let's go."

We both sprang out of the car, and as we approached the job site, I saw Razor standing calmly at the entrance. "Get to work." His voice was cool and clear. It helped to settle the nerves jumping around in my stomach.

I pulled out my tool kit and jimmied the top and bottom locks open. I had them open within fifteen seconds. Then I carefully put my tools away. As we walked in, I found the safe in the back closet under the food and coffee items, just as Lynn had explained. The safe was exactly like the one I'd studied in Lynn's pictures. I laid out my tools on the floor, remembering Nikki's saying about believing what you are. Sucking in a deep breath, I thought, *I am a professional*.

The safe had two locks, a keypad and a physical key lock. First, I popped the top panel off to reveal the computer grid. I attached the electronic receiver and tripped the wires to bypass the code. It worked. Step one complete. Now for the key. I shimmied the lock pick and quickly found the weakness in the mechanism, for every lock had a weakness. It was easier than I'd expected, and the lock yielded within five seconds. I opened it to find the stack of cash waiting for me. Before I reached for it, I meticulously put away my tools. I wouldn't want anyone to find them and trace this back to me.

Quickly, I removed the cash and stuffed it into the duffel bag I carried in with me. There was still some cash left and as I turned back to the safe to reach for it a shiny object caught my eye in the back. I squinted my eyes.

It was a golden, iced-out Rolex. Worth more than I could even imagine.

I looked around the room as I contemplated my next move. Razor was still at the entrance. He glanced at me and I quickly dropped my gaze to the duffle bag, shoving more money in. The second he glanced back out the door I grabbed it and stuffed it into my bra. *Consider this my bonus*, I thought, and smiled to myself. I shoved the remaining cash into the bag and then closed the safe. I placed everything back exactly where I'd found it and walked out of the building.

Elio exhaled deeply as I returned to the car and slid into the back seat. The second Razor closed his door in the front passenger seat, we pulled out of our tucked-away parking spot. The calming sound of silence in the air was soothing, especially since I expected to hear the loud sirens chasing after us by now. Razor took off his cap, and we all followed suit. He turned to look at me. "You did good Sasha, real good."

"Thanks," I replied, my eyes shifting quickly.

I was glad he thought so, but his words didn't calm me. Pins still pierced my stomach as we drove, and the cool metal of the watch in my bra burned against my skin. I kept looking through the back window of the minivan for tails, but there weren't any.

When we got back to his house, I carried in the bag and opened it up on the table. There were three large stacks of money that I guessed amounted to ten thousand dollars each. Not bad at all for thirty minutes of work.

Elio smiled broadly and slid his arm around me. "You make me proud, *Estrellita."* He used using his nickname for me, and hugged me close.

We celebrated with music, drink, and smokes at Razor's, but I couldn't get in the mood. I was wound up in thoughts about the watch in my bra and the police walking in on us at any moment—maybe they'd tailed us from the job site. They could be sitting outside right now, waiting for their moment to burst in and arrest us all. I stood by the window, peering through the blinds out to the street and squinting to see if there were bodies in the cars sitting idle in the driveways. I felt a warm presence behind me, almost brushing against my skin, and turned my head up to meet Elio's dark eyes.

"Hey." He smiled down at me as though I held an answer to a question he wanted to ask.

A surge of excitement coursed through me at his proximity, and I wanted to ignore it, but I couldn't. "Hey." I returned his gaze with a slight crinkle in my brow.

"Hey, hey... It's ok. I know you haven't done this before. We're good, ok? What? Are you looking for cops outside?" He let out a breathy laugh at the thought, releasing the sweet smell of whisky and spice from his lips.

I bowed my head and shuffled my feet in embarrassment. "I want to get home..." I was ready to put an end to this night.

He seemed light and airy as a cool breeze in the summer. The dark scowl he normally wore to intimidate his customers was absent now. "Are you sure you want to go home, *estrellita*?" His eyes were warm as they searched mine. His short, black beard was trimmed neatly, accentuating his dark features. The scent of cedarwood and sage wafted into my nostrils, and I bit down on my lower lip.

He leaned in closer, his hands sliding up my arms, up toward my face.

He cradled my jaw in his hand and pulled me in to meet his lips. We'd just broken through the friend zone. I pushed against him, his muscles unyielding against my hands and my face melting into his embrace. He kissed me with everything, and his teeth felt smooth against my tongue. My arms reached up and around his neck, and the tightness in my legs relaxed in his warm embrace. He pulled back, his familiar face comforting and his eyes lit with desire.

A warmth grew within me, and I wanted him to consume me. I wanted to feel his hands everywhere, up my stomach, my back, my thighs. I needed to taste his caramel neck and feel his chest against my lips. I wanted to touch every part of him, and his hands told me they wanted to do the same.

But being with Elio might mean losing him. He might start to see me as just another girl he'd slept with. I had to be more to him than that. I couldn't risk losing him. He was one of the few people I could count on in this world.

"I should go…" I whispered.

His hand reached down from my face and touched my bra where the watch was. There was something about the way he did it that told me he knew it was there. He caught me completely off guard; I had forgotten about the watch.

His eyes darkened as he squeezed the fabric and felt for it. "Sasha, what the fuck?" The corners of his eyes crinkled and his mouth opened in disbelief. A grimace returned to his face.

I tried to smile, to make light of it like it was no big deal. I slowly slid it out of its place in my bra and handed it to him.

He turned the watch in his hand and examined its jewels. "You could get shot for stealing from Razor. Are you fucking crazy?" he hissed between tight teeth. His expression darkened.

"He only said he wanted the money. He never said anything about a watch. I found it, so it's mine." I snatched it back out of his hand.

He reached for my hand and gripped it so tight I felt the blood stop circulating. I squirmed under his grasp and released the watch into his open palm. He stole a glance behind him, and to both our satisfaction, no one seemed to notice our scuffle.

He spoke again in a low and steady voice. "Those were not the terms. You're just like your father." His face turned cold and he slid the watch into his pocket. Then he turned and walked away.

Up until this point I had trusted Elio with my life, but now I knew all he cared about was his ambition. My blood boiled as hot as molten rock, a fire burning bright inside my chest. I'd just messed up my chance with the mafia, and now I'd be treated like my father. My soul was ripping while my lips were still tingling from his kiss. I reached my fingers up to touch them and winced from their heat.

I had fifteen hundred dollars in cash in my pocket, more money than I had ever possessed at one time. I could finally afford to grab an Uber. I snatched my tools and walked out the front door to get myself home. But I didn't want to go home.

I texted Nikki and luckily, she texted back. I headed over to crash at her house for the night. That night, I had the strangest dream...

Endless views of tropical mountains flooded my mind as I looked out from the high balcony of a luxury hotel. As I gazed, soaking in the pristine sunrise, a chill rose up the back of my neck. The chill got more intense, so I looked behind me and watched in awe as the hotel room shifted from luxury accommodations to a neglected one-star room.

With the shift in space came whispers on a bristly, dark wind, shrouding the furniture in a dim shadow. Panicking, I looked for an exit, then remembered I could fly. I turned away, ready to fly from the balcony, but I seemed to be stuck. Metal shackles kept me in place, gripping my ankles tightly. Helpless, I trembled with the realization that I couldn't move.

Fire began to stir beneath my skin, like a beast clawing at me from the inside, wishing to be released. I was now ready to face my captor and attack. When I lifted my gaze, my bones froze where they stood.

The menacing darkness inched closer with every breath. It rattled and slithered toward me, covering the walls as a solid black form crept forward. I yanked at the shackles, searching for an escape as the tiniest drops of perspiration dripped from my forehead. Within seconds, my hair was completely drenched in sweat.

Tugging on the shackles was hopeless, and the black form grew from the walls into a forest of dark, intertangled bodies reaching out to grab me. Scarred and bloodied arms tried to pull me in with them.

I curled into a ball as a fire grew within me, a rising heat kindled by the rage of feeling cornered, trapped, and helpless, my power ripped from me.

I looked up as a single clawed hand reached to touch the tip of my knee. When it grazed my skin, it glowed and sizzled, burning from the touch.

On instinct, I reached out my hand and shot a fierce blaze of fire directly at the Shadow and all of its beasts. A deep red flame released, and those gruesome creatures stepped closer into the fire I had thrown. They grew within the fire and stood up, even stronger and fiercer than before.

I screamed with fear and pain, jerking myself awake.

CHAPTER TEN

Nikki looked at me with sleepy eyes from her own bed. "Hey, you ok?"

I touched my soaked lace tank top and looked around the room, searching for a dark shadow that I couldn't find. Once relief set in that I was no longer in the nightmare, I got up to change my shirt and wipe myself off.

Nikki shifted in her bed, and asked in a soft voice, "Was that another one of your shadow dreams?"

"Cabrón." I said out loud, but Nikki knew that was on reflex. "Yes, it was, and I am so over it." Nikki was fully versed in my nightmares. I told her each time I'd have one.

It was when I walked into the bathroom that I noticed my knee was hurting. I had a thin burn about three inches long on top of the knee cap. How was that even possible? This wasn't normal.

"Hey, you ok?" Nikki whispered sleepily.

"No, I'm not. I just don't understand..." My mind wandered.

"Talk to mami tomorrow. She can help you." She shifted in her bed and pulled her blankets around her. Unlike her, I couldn't find my way to sleep. I lay awake, thinking about the shackles on my ankles. The burn on my skin. The strangeness of it all. The next morning, I quickly jumped out of bed as the first rays of light entered the room. It was a lazy Saturday, and her mother happened to be home. She made us breakfast, and I couldn't help but notice that she snuck sudden glances my way.

I was about to ask her why when Nikki said brightly, "I've got some news. I'm moving in with my dad in New York at the end of the month."

"What? Nikki! No, you can't go." I didn't intend to sound so disturbed. She must be desperate. An intense pressure resounded in my head, and I felt like it was about to explode.

"Yeah, my dad said he'll pay for me to go to school. I want to study visual arts and filmography. Mami wants me to go, don't you?" She turned to her mother, who was sitting on a large, round wicker chair surrounded by colorful pillows.

"Yes," she replied, but her eyes were still distant, watching me closely.

"I can't believe you're telling me all this, now—like this." The fire I'd felt in my chest yesterday returned and stirred upon itself, kindling even more heat. She wouldn't even listen to what I had to say about this. What did I have, if not her?

"Come with me, then."

Well, that was an option. The thought of getting the hell out of my parents' and going with her soothed the heat that blazed within my chest, and I relaxed my shoulders just a bit.

"Ha, I wish. I can't afford New York." I shuddered at the thought that I was losing her.

I had just fallen out with Elio, and now she was leaving. I would be alone. Nikki had her own life to live, and it sounded like she would have a chance to make something of it, which was more than I had. As much as I wanted her to stay, I couldn't make her.

I was still wrapping my head around everything when Ms. Gabriel came to me. "Sasha, come and talk to me for a minute." Nikki had already picked up her phone and started texting with someone.

I joined Ms. Gabriel in her small living room, surrounded by macramé, ceramics and pillows that all had a rustic, earthy feel to them.

"How are you feeling lately?" she asked. "Is something going on with you, something different?"

"It's the zodiac dreams. Last night I found this burn on my knee and in my dream, I'd burned myself with a fire that came from my own fingers. I don't understand any of it." I shook my head in disbelief and showed her my knee. I didn't sense a hint of surprise as she inspected it, then looked at my hands.

"I had a strange dream about you, too," she explained, eyes wide with concern. "I had a vision of you wrapped in fire while chained to the floor. I was looking for you, but I couldn't find you."

"I had a dream that I was wrapped in fire a few nights ago." I shook my head and raised my eyebrows in confusion.

She shrugged sympathetically. "I wish I knew."

"The sun is in my chart." I only mumbled this, as if that had something to do with it.

"And you're an Aries, right?"

I nodded.

"You must be channeling the fire element. Work on your breathing to calm your mind, mija. You don't want the fire to consume you. Instead, you want to control it."

What she didn't know was that it was already consuming me, and controlling it was the hardest thing I'd ever done.

"Tell me more about the dreams."

"Well, I call them the zodiac shadow dreams. Because in almost every dream I end up near a gate of some kind with a zodiac sign at the top of it."

"Dreams are just our subconscious way of processing all the things that happened to us, to help us make sense of it in our conscious life," she said this as if having these kinds of dreams was the most normal thing in the world.

She cradled the mug in her hands and took a long sip, then went on, "Every element of the dream is a projection of a part of ourselves. Our minds used images, symbols, and even other people to help us relate and explore the complexities we experienced in our waking lives. So, those zodiac shadows are a part of you, and if you want to learn more about what they mean you need to learn more about what the shadows represent in your dreams."

As of right now, all I saw was fear.

"Will you do a reading for me, please?"

"Are you sure? Sometimes it's better if your path remains hidden." Her eyes were round and her brows creased.

"I need to know what these shadows mean. I can't keep guessing." My jaw tightened.

She walked over to her cabinet to retrieve the cards and sat back down. She set them out on the coffee table, one by one in front of me using the Celtic Cross Card Spread. In the tenth card position, which is gives sight to the outcome of my situation, she turned up the Devil card. Her hand trembled as she pulled it back. I winced.

"Let's do it again." I wasn't going to so quickly accept that these shadows meant violence, seduction, fatality, and predestined evil. I watched her shuffle the deck with great care. I split the deck myself and selected the cards that she would turn and place in the cross. Again, for the tenth card, she turned up the Devil.

"So that's it then, I'm cursed." My hands surged with heat and I turned my head away from Ms. Gabriel. I stared out her window at the palm trees that stood motionless outside.

"Perhaps. And perhaps the cards just want to prepare you for the challenges you will face."

"You mean the challenges I am facing." I scowled as I kept my eyes locked on the palm tree outside.

"No, I won't lie to you Sasha. I sense there is a lot more to all of this. What you are facing now is only the beginning. Get strong and be ready. There is more to come."

Chapter Eleven

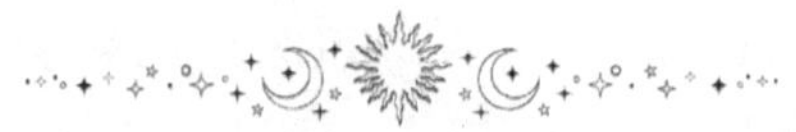

At the end of the month, Nikki left, and we threw a small going away party at her mother's house. Although my throat was tight and tears welled just beneath the surface, I smiled, hugged her and wished her well. I got her one of those silly best-friend-forever necklaces as a joke. She loved it and packed it away in her suitcase.

She turned to me one last time, and when I saw a tear spill from her eye, I knew I could release mine. We agreed that we were being silly and we would video chat every day or almost every day.

It was my nineteenth birthday just a few days later, and I felt so utterly alone. Elio and I hadn't spoken since the night of the Rolex. I called him anyway; I wanted to put it behind us.

"Hey, what are getting you up to? Did you forget?" I asked him.

"No, I didn't forget. Happy Birthday, nena. You know I love you, but you messed up." His voice was raw and cold.

I scowled. This conversation was starting to annoy me. "Look, you got the watch. Fine, I messed up. I'm sorry, all right?"

"Razor knew it was in there, and you were the dumbass who failed his test. He won't hire you again, and now you put my reputation on the line. If I had let you keep it, he never would have hired me again, either. Look, Sasha, everyone expects you to fuck up because of your father. All you did was prove him right. I'm the only reason they didn't give you a beatdown that night. But now you're just making me look bad."

That information hit me like a brick over the head.

"Fuck Razor." My face flushed, and my heart pounded in my chest. This was all kinds of wrong.

"I knew you weren't ready. Look, whatever. I know it's your birthday. What are you doing?"

I was pissed at this whole situation, but I couldn't stay home tonight. I was getting restless and I couldn't stand the thought of being alone. It was all I could do to stop thinking about the zodiac shadows that would be coming for me. I needed to get out.

"Nothing. Come get me? Nikki left for New York and it sucks." I swallowed hard, feeling pretty low right about now.

There was a long silence on the other line. I wondered if he was considering if he should still be upset with me.

"Yeah, I need to talk to you anyway." I could tell he was being careful not to speak about anything criminal on the phone. "So, let's celebrate. We can be there like around nine. Meet us at the end of the block; I don't want to pull up in your driveway."

"Ok, where are we going?"

"We can go to my friend's house," he answered. "He'll have some drinks, and we can chill."

"All right, see you then." After I hung up, I called my cousin Olga to see if she wanted to come, but she didn't answer. At eight-thirty I got ready to head out.

Tonight, I'm treating them to a good smoke, I thought.

I knew these guys would appreciate it. I hit up my stash and took out half a pound of weed in a Ziploc and put it into my purse, along with papers and a lighter. One of my Jamaican friends had given me about three pounds of extra-dry ganja that he'd asked me to sell for him, but I knew it was barely worth anything at all because of how dry it was. It was ok to smoke, but no one would buy this junk off me, so I might as well bring it tonight and give it away to whoever was around.

As I headed out the front door, I yelled behind me, "I'm going out." Then I walked down the block to a black lowrider with bass booming from the back seat, and Elio looked over at me with a slanted smile. Three other young men who I didn't know welcomed me into the car.

I slowed my pace as I approached and stopped before opening the door. I stared at the handle. Maybe this wasn't such a good idea.

From outside, I heard their conversations, and suddenly a strong ringing pierced my ears. A screech rang out in the night sky, and it sounded to me like an unnatural high-pitched scream. I shook my head. *This was not normal. I hope I'm not losing my mind.* It quickly passed, and I opened the door and got in.

The guy in the front passenger seat had gold teeth glinting from his huge grin. He gave me a sideways look. "What's up, shorty? How you doin'?"

"Oh, I'm good, thanks." He was new. I'd never met him before. He had a snake tattooed on his neck and from what I could tell his arms and hands were covered.

"It's her nineteenth birthday," Elio told him.

"Well, then happy birthday to the birthday girl." He chuckled.

"Thanks," I answered.

The lowrider spurred to a start and had reached about ten miles an hour only a few feet from where they'd picked me up when we heard sirens behind us. I thought about the weed in my purse. What was I going to do with this contraband? If I dropped it in the car, Elio would go to jail. If I shoved it in my pants, they might not search me or find it at all.

It would be just my luck to get arrested on my birthday. When I was sixteen, I'd gotten arrested for shoplifting and had to do twenty community hours at the local library, spending hours cataloging books while getting the evil eye from the librarians. I'd been charged as a juvenile, but now I would be treated like an adult if they found the dried-up, worthless stash.

One by one, they lined us up on the concrete sidewalk. Mr. Gold Teeth was immediately arrested. The cop merely motioned for me to sit as he and his partner continued to question Elio and his friends.

I waited on the rough, cool sidewalk, aimlessly watching their footsteps—and the slightest facial gesture or move of a hand—while the sounds of the nearby crickets pounded in my ears.

The two officers were just standing there talking like they were gathered around a water cooler when another police car pulled up. A female officer got out and nodded at the other officers as she walked directly to me.

Any hope of getting out of this situation unscathed withered away when she said, "Ok, stand up. Now place your hands out to your sides like this."

As I did, she patted me down. The closer she came to my crotch, the more I realized this wouldn't be good. She smiled when she felt the foreign object hidden against my thigh. "Ok, take it on out. You just wasted my time making me come all the way down here when you should have just fessed up from the beginning. Do you have a medical card for this?" I shook my head.

Elio's face darkened, then I believe I saw him soften just a little.

I mouthed, "I'm sorry," and he turned his head away.

Without another word from any of them, the young male officer handed me a piece of paper and told me to walk home. I later learned this meant I had been arrested but released on my own recognizance and had to show up in court. When I got to the house, I balled up the stupid pink paper. I went to the cabinet and poured myself a tall glass of rum and Coke.

Happy effing birthday to me.

I went back to my room and sat on my bed, reconsidering my pathetic life choices when the high-pitched screech pierced my ears once again.

I stood, pacing the room, and covered my ears with my hands to muffle the sound. My eyes squeezed shut in a grimace from the pain, and when I opened them ever so slightly, I witnessed the room covered with the black haze of my dreams.

Was I dreaming? Had I fallen asleep? This felt more real than any dream could feel. The haze covered every inch of my flesh and encompassed my entire body.

I waved my arms wildly at my sides and tried to shake it off, but all I saw was the black mist. Electrical pulses charged straight into my pores. The whispers of damned souls resounded even louder in my ears. When I opened my mouth to scream, the only thing that left my throat was a soft whimper. I could only see black as the mist covered my eyes and the electric charges that surrounded me stung my skin. I squeezed them tight and opened them once again. As I did, I saw the mist soaking into my very flesh.

The Shadow was inside me. And truth be told, I didn't hate it. Not entirely. It was a strange kind of power that rocked me from within and surged through me. Yet, my mind began to race. I couldn't hold a thought. Everything felt as though it was everywhere and as the darkness filled my body and mind, I felt incredibly lost. Beyond lost and beyond afraid I couldn't get back.

I didn't sleep for the rest of the night. As the days past my mind began to return to me and I sent whispers to the universe for those shadows to never return.

A week later, I was sitting on a picnic table at college when I got a 911 text from my mother. I called her back, and she was frantic.

"Sasha, I'm going to kill you. I opened a letter from the city because it looked official, and it says you have a warrant out for your arrest because you missed a court date?"

My heart dropped. Suddenly everything around me sounded loud, and the campus seemed more crowded than it did before I'd gotten on the phone with her.

"Oh yeah, don't worry about that. It's not a big deal. I'll take care of it." I did my best to sound nonchalant, sarcastic, and in control. The truth was, I had forgotten all about it.

"You better!" she yelled back.

The day of my hearing, the judge said that because there were no priors on my record, I would only be sentenced to thirty hours of community service. Upon completion of the hours, the charges would be dropped, and the records sealed.

My eyes watered as I walked out of the courtroom. I found myself right back to having to do community service hours. All the way home from the courthouse, I thought about how I kept getting myself into these situations. Why did I always find a way to mess everything up?

Just as I was kicking myself for being an ass, I got the kind of pep talk no one ever needs from the last friend I had left in Miami.

I sent Elio a text. *You still aren't talking to me?*

I'd sent him several texts over the past week, and he'd never responded to any. This time he finally wrote back.

I don't have anything to say.

Come on, Elio, it's not that big a deal.

I can't sit back and watch you fuck up your life just like your father.

That stung, but now I knew why he was avoiding me, and the crazy part was, I knew he was right. I kept thinking about his message when I arrived home and lay down on my bed. I was tired. After all, going downtown to the courthouse and getting sentenced wasn't something I did every day. I shut my eyes to sleep, and when I awoke, I wrote down this dream.

I found myself in a busy area of a huge public park. It might have been a national park. The family dog that'd died years before, King, was with me, and I was taking him for a walk. I remembered how much I'd loved walking him and having some downtime away from the chaos at the house.

As I walked him, I saw a familiar gate with an absurdly massive crimson archway, and it was intricately decorated with what appeared to be gods and mythological creatures ready for battle.

I had seen this in a dream before.

It reminded me of the overwhelming size of the Arc de Triomphe in Paris that I'd seen on the Travel Channel. The gate had a single symbol carved into the stone at the very top: the Aries ram with long, curved horns at the sides. The gate appeared to lead into a sectioned-off part of the park.

Beyond the gate, a group of jaguars lurked in the trees, ready to pounce on the passersby below them. Something about that group of jaguars intrigued me. Weren't they solitary creatures? What were they doing hanging out together like that? As soon as I saw them, I heard buzzing whispers and then a high-pitched screeching of a thousand voices, changing in cadence and tone, faintly in the background.

A man stood at the entrance of the gate, a stranger with thick wavy hair and eyes that looked as if they were carved from stone. "You shouldn't go that way. Those jaguars would love to eat your beautiful dog."

He was probably right, but if I didn't go, I wouldn't get to see the park. All those people walking by weren't being killed, so why would we? Another voice crept up from inside me, a still voice much like my own. "He is who you seek."

Now who the hell is in my head? Am I so fucking broken that I have voices in my head? Then an image of the magician tarot card flashed in my mind and I knew this was my shaman.

I searched his eyes, but they remained cold and wavering. I scowled at him and went ahead anyway. Shaman or not, I'm not letting you stop me.

The jaguars became alert to our presence, and as I walked toward them, the sounds got louder.

One minute it was bright daylight, and the next it turned to night. The jaguars lurked in slow, calculated movements as I walked down the path and passed their tree. They crouched on branches while they studied their daring new visitors. From fifty feet away, I became instinctively aware that if I took one step closer to these animals, they would leap and devour both King and me.

In an instant, I turned and ran as fast as I could, back toward the gate at the entrance. When I reached the gate, the same man with a sly grin was there to open it. After we'd exited, he quickly closed the gate, and I realized the jaguars had jumped off the tree and chased us. They were directly behind the gate when the man had closed it.

We'd almost been devoured.

"You can't enter the Gates yet," he said. "You aren't ready."

Chapter Twelve

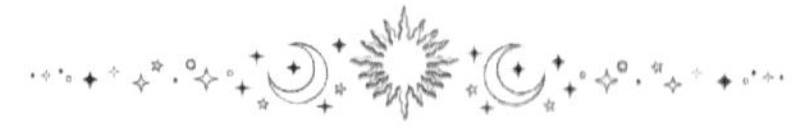

The day was unusually cold for South Florida. Thick gray clouds covered the entire sky as I scampered out of my house in a sweater, jeans, and sneakers. Before I got on the bus to work, I took a deep breath of the fresh, cool air, The day was such a contrast from the sticky, humid Florida heat I was used to.

The Shadow continued to visit my dreams in one way or another, and at times during the day, I thought I could hear its whisper. The same buzz ringing in my ears that unsettled my sleep also fogged my thinking during the day. I desperately wanted it to go away, but I couldn't seem to figure out how to make it leave me alone. Sometimes I would picture myself leaving this town, the monotony of the day-to-day life in the same place. Maybe then I would stop hearing this torturous sound and feeling its presence.

I arrived early to campus and was sitting at a table, sorting through my assignments for the day, when I noticed a man just steps away from me. I raked my eyes along his body. "What, are you a student now?" I asked with a smile creeping onto my lips.

"I'm considering it." Omar laughed and sat in the empty chair next to me. His knee brushed up against mine.

I felt myself simmer with petals of heat creeping up into my chest. Having him this close made my heart race. Just when I had almost forgotten about him, he was back.

He tilted his head to one side. "I was enrolling in a class and saw you sitting here. Looking the way you do, I had to come by and say hello."

I pursed my lips at his compliment, crossing my legs and turning from my books to face him. He seemed even more completely put together than the last time I saw him.

"Well, I hope you can at least try to avoid getting into a fight this time." I smirked and cocked my head.

"No promises, but I will try. I never deleted your number, though." He grinned just like the bad boy he was. Apparently he wasn't worried about causing more issues with Elio. "Let me take you out tonight. We could go somewhere nice for dinner."

All I had to look forward to eating tonight was a frozen dinner in my mother's freezer. Elio had stopped talking to me, but you know what? I didn't owe him anything. I wasn't mafia, and he clearly didn't want me around anymore. Plus, he thought I was just like my father, and I couldn't stand that about him. *Pendejo.*

"Ok, yeah. I'd like that. Can you pick me up at nine-thirty?"

"You bet. See you then." When he gave me his one-dimpled smile, I knew this night had potential.

He smelled and looked as fresh as a spring shower when I entered his car later that evening. We were seated at an outdoor table by the ocean, taking in the majestic views of the bay.

After some light conversation, Omar asked me, "So I heard you did a job for Razor. Is it true?"

I looked off into the dark horizon; it was decorated with light-gray clouds, and the tips of the tranquil waves glowed silver. Then I returned his gaze. I had to be honest with him. "Yes, it's true."

"So, are you mafia or what?"

"No." I shook my head. "I'm just a girl in school. I did one job and never spoke to any of them again."

It was the truth... even though I'd left out the details. I didn't want to get into the fact that I'd failed one of the stupid mafia tests, then got myself arrested with Elio on my birthday, and that Elio wasn't speaking to me because he didn't want my messy life to block him from his mafia-king goals.

"Good." He seemed pleased.

We went out several more times, and I began to think we were becoming a couple. He would pick me up from work some nights, and sometimes he would just show up at my house unannounced. There were nights we would just hang out at his house, order in, and watch movies. But it was when we went to the zoo together that we really had something to talk about. Estaba bien cabrón.

As we arrived at the ticket booth, the attendant gave us our tickets and a map and said, "I hear the jaguar is unusually awake and moving around today, causing quite a stir. If you have any fears of big cats, you might want to avoid that exhibit."

We both looked at each other and smiled, knowing exactly where we were headed.

When we approached the jaguar exhibit, a group of about ten visitors were crowded by the viewing point, watching intently. As we got closer, we saw an all-black jaguar pacing back and forth, back and forth. Then I heard a sound—that screeching whisper from my Shadow dreams.

My eyes searched the crowd, wondering if that annoying-as-fuck Shadow was nearby. I'd never told Omar about my nightmares, as I figured they would go away at some point. When I reached to grab Omar's hand, the jaguar stopped pacing. It sniffed the air and looked around. At first, I didn't remember my dream about the jaguars, but then it hit me like a fierce blow of wind that comes out of nowhere.

I let go of Omar's hand, and as if by reflex, I approached the deep canal and fences lined with bushes that separated us from the creature. The jaguar turned and roared, exposing her four sharp fangs, and the crowd let out a nervous laugh. She flicked her deep emerald eyes toward mine, and we locked gazes as she took calculated, lurking steps toward me. I sensed Omar watching this all take place in awe.

For several heartbeats the jaguar and I both just stood there, staring at each other. Her hair was as black as mine, her eyes the same shade of green. Then the creature crouched down, ready to spring. Omar grabbed my arms and swept me out of the area before I could blink.

"Yo, ok so what was that?" Omar asked as he pulled me toward him. The sharp lines of his muscles pressing against my arm and side.

"I don't... know." I managed to blurt out. My brows pinched at the center and my eyes flashed back and forth as I tried to understand if this happened in real life or a dream. Omar let out a deep laugh as he drew me closer toward him. We approached a tree-lined walkway that led to an unoccupied covered rest area. As we entered, he pressed me against a column and rested his arm on the wooden structure behind me. I leaned back on it then let out a deep sigh. He brushed the hair from my neck as he inspected my bare skin.

"Is there something I should know about you? Are you a jaguar whisperer or something?" His eyes danced as his sensuous lips drew closer to mine. I stared at his mouth for far longer than normal.

"Ha, maybe I am." I lifted my hands to his chest and felt those firm lines under my palms. I bit my bottom lip as warmth began to pool between my legs.

Before I could say anything else his lips were on mine and he pressed them against me. I arched my back in response. His teeth grazed my flesh and his tongue searched for mine. He kept his body separated though, and I reached my other hand up and around his waist then I fisted his shirt. He pulled back from our kiss and looked at me. His other hand made its way around my waist then he whispered in my ear.

"That shit back there kind of shook me, but I liked it."

He bit his bottom lip now as his eyes bored into mine.

"Let's get out of here." I began to walk away and pulled him behind me as I went. He followed with a quick step and draped his arm around my shoulder as the noise and crowds faded behind us.

Chapter Thirteen

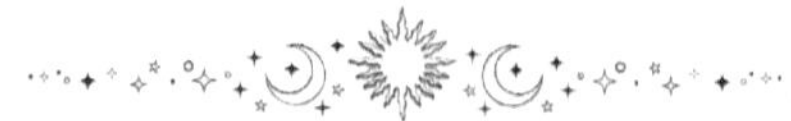

Nikki had come down from New York to visit her mother, and later that evening, I called her. "Hey, I need to talk to your mom about my dreams. They're coming true."

"Ok, are you high right now? What do you mean?"

I explained my dream about the jaguars I'd seen in the tree, and then about what had happened at the zoo.

She yelled, "Mami... You need to talk to Sasha now!"

Ms. Gabriel had come to Miami as a teenager in one of the many Freedom Flights when Fidel Castro had announced that Cubans wishing to emigrate could do so. She'd then moved to California with her family and grew up around New Age spiritualists that'd introduced her to astrology, yoga and the presence of spiritual energy in all things.

This may have been why I found her so different from all the other religious parents I'd grown up around. She was easy to talk to and not at all judgey.

She listened carefully as I told her what had happened and asked me questions like, "How did that make you feel?" and, "What was going through your mind when you locked eyes with the big cat?" When I finished, she gave me an exceptionally long explanation, telling me I should open myself up to the possibility that I may have psychic abilities through my dreams.

I felt my chest sink in and a haunted heaviness wash over me. "Ms. Gabriel, what are you saying, exactly?"

"I believe you can see events, like visions of things that happen, taking place in the future. It is not that uncommon, especially in dreams. They call it precognition. Why don't you come over tomorrow and I can balance your chakras to clear any energy blockages that are keeping you from being at peace? I can teach you how to do this for yourself, too."

I caught a glimpse of my reflection in the mirror. My eyebrows were furrowed at the middle, and my long black hair was slightly disheveled. My focus blurred as I saw my reflection, and where my face was, I saw the black jaguar. Her deep green eyes stared at me once again, the image burned inside my mind. With a cracked voice I told her, "Ok, yeah, sure. I can be there after you get home from work."

Ms. Gabriel received me at the door barefoot, wearing a long silk cardigan with an Asian-flower print, a white tank top and jeans underneath. I left my shoes at the door, as I always did, and she welcomed me in.

"Nikki laid down for a nap just a little while ago. I didn't wake her so that you and I could have some privacy." She went to the kitchen, and I followed after.

I watched as she poured what appeared to be hot water into a large mug. She picked up a string hanging from the cup and lifted it up and down in the water. I moved to sit at the kitchen table.

"So, are you still dreaming of the fire?" she asked me when we were settled.

"Yeah, it feels like a kind of message from my dreams that I can't seem to shake. I'm always surrounded by fire, and sometimes I can shoot it from my hands at these creatures in my dreams. What does that mean?" I knew it was wild to expect her to just answer this kind of question, but I had to start somewhere.

She scrunched her eyebrows, intrigued by the thought. "It could mean a lot of things. Like maybe you're taking out your frustration on these creatures that seem to want to hurt you. And maybe the creatures represent the people in your life, like your father or Elio."

"It could be, but it feels like much more than that."

"When is your birthday?" She also wanted the exact time and location.

"Oh, are you going to run my natal chart?" Thanks to Lily, I already had my natal chart memorized, and all of the information it held about the alignment of each of the planets in their journey around the Sun at the time of my birth.

"Yes, I am."

I didn't want to tell her how familiar I already was with it in case she noticed anything new or different.

She went to her computer and pulled up the familiar circular chart with all its colorful lines and tiny shapes placed within the circle. "See, those are the symbols for the twelve houses of the zodiac. This one that looks like a curved *V* is your sign, Aries, and it is said to be ruled by the god of war, Ares. Of his many powers, fire was his favorite, and he was said to burst a city into flames with the unsheathing of his blade. See this circle with a tiny dot in the middle? That's the sun. It's in the first house. This tells me that fire is strong in your birth chart."

"Yes, I see that." I remembered much of this from my own studies of the zodiac, but it didn't explain why the fire sign was so amped up now.

She seemed to notice my thoughtful expression. "It's a lot, right? These lines and shapes all mean different things. But take a look at this." She pointed at a strange symbol on the chart. "That is the North Node, and it is in Scorpio, meaning in this life you will go through a series of transformations and you will have to accept that change is the only constant. However, seeing this"—she now pointed at a few numbers and lines—"your Black Moon Lilith is in Pisces. This tells me you can tap into other dimensions, which could explain your dreams and premonitions.

"Our society has never been open to these concepts, which will make it hard for you to talk about what you are seeing and feeling with other people. They won't understand, and many times people with this planetary lineup fall into addictions, alcohol, sex, and drugs to cope with their perception of reality. Be careful, ok?"

My chest felt heavy at the realization that this was exactly what was happening to me.

"Don't worry." She laughed, probably trying to ease me out of my tense expression. "Mediation will help, and so will clearing your chakras. Come, sit on these." She motioned me toward the large, colorful floor pillows with mandala embroidery all around. "Now, I want you to sit with your feet flat on the floor and your back straight. Let's take three deep breaths in through our nose"—she inhaled—"and out through our mouths."

She exhaled for what felt like five long seconds. We did this three times. She then walked me through a process of scanning my body, from my feet to the top of my head, and had me acknowledge any sensations I felt or did not feel. When all this was completed, she taught me about chakras.

Ms. Gabriel explained that there are seven main chakras related to the energy we have in our bodies, and they each connect to a specific set of nerve bundles. It all sounded kind of wild, but at this point, I was willing to give anything a try. I listened closely as she explained and even took notes.

"Each of the chakras is associated with a specific color and a stone. The root chakra is at the base of our spine; its color is red." She placed a red stone in front of me. "When this energy is flowing well, it will help you feel grounded and able to withstand challenges. The sacral chakra is located just below the belly button, and its color is orange. It is intricately linked with your emotions and the emotions of others." She removed an orange stone from a small cloth satchel and placed it next to the red one. "The solar plexus chakra's color is yellow, and it is important for feeling in control of your life. It is in the stomach area and is responsible for self-confidence and self-esteem." She placed a yellow stone on the table.

She moved her hand to her chest and continued, "The heart chakra is in the center of your chest, near your heart, and relates to your ability to show love and compassion. Its color is green." She removed a rose-colored stone and placed it on the table next to the others.

"If the chakra is green, why is the stone's color rose?"

"There are many different stones that can be used for each chakra. The important thing is not the colors, but the elements possessed by the crystals or stones themselves. Rose quartz is the stone of unconditional love and brings the most healing to our hearts.

"Now on to the throat chakra. This is all about how you communicate. Its color is light blue." She removed a turquoise stone and gently placed it in the line.

Then she lifted her hand to her forehead. "The sixth chakra is the third eye chakra. It's right here. Its color is indigo." She pressed lightly on the space between her eyes, then removed a deep blue stone and placed it next in the line. "When this is open, you will have a strong intuition, enhancing your ability to perceive the more subtle aspects of our living reality and the movements of energy. And finally, you have the crown chakra, up here. Its color can be white or violet." She touched the top of her head, then placed a shiny white stone on the table. "When you open this up, you will fully connect with your spirituality. Now let's clear all this blocked energy, shall we?"

She had me lay down on the couch while she knelt on one of her big throw pillows right next to me. She placed the different colored stones on each chakra, starting with the root chakra, and as she did, she told me to hum a specific sound for two minutes each time. After the second hum, I started to fidget.

"Sasha, what's going on? You need to keep still."

"Ok, ok. Just, how much longer are we doing this?"

"You can stop now, if you want. I've got other things to do." She sat back on her heels, looking annoyed.

"Sorry, um, no. No, it's ok. I'm sorry. I would like to finish."

When we got to the heart chakra, a deep sadness swelled in my chest, and I felt the pain of Titi Lily's death wash over me once again. After I'd lost Titi Lily, the relationship with my mother had also changed, and I'd never truly acknowledged how much that'd hurt me until right at this moment. Elio's face flashed in my mind and my stomach felt empty, hollow. I missed him. Nikki was next; I pictured us laughing together over pancakes at her mom's house. Warm tears released from my eyes, and I took in a deep, calming breath. After a few of these, my entire body relaxed.

Ms. Gabriel seemed to notice since she took her time now and moved more slowly into the third eye chakra. As soon as I repeated the humming sound she was making, I began to see bright colors everywhere: vibrant flashes of electric purple, indigo, red, blue, yellow, orange and green intertwined with whites and splashes of charcoal and black. It was like a fireworks show in my mind, and as I watched it in deep relaxation, the corners of my mouth lifted into a serene smile.

We moved to the final chakra, the crown. At this stage, I felt my body and mind become firm and strong. Unbreakable.

The man from my jaguar dream appeared to me again in this deep state of meditation. He was holding his hand out with a flame glowing brightly from it. The flame grew brighter and stronger. He spoke a single word, and the flame shot toward me. A warm fire covered my entire body, but my skin didn't burn.

From fifty feet away, I heard my own voice whisper on the breeze. *In order to survive your transformation, you will have to find him.*

Ding. In the background, I heard the unfamiliar sound of a bell.

Ms. Gabriel's voice sounded faraway. "When you are ready, you can open your eyes."

I opened my eyes and looked around the room. Was Nikki's house always this earthy? It was as if every statue, colorful vase, or macramé hanging on the walls had some deeper purpose or a meaning behind it. Slowly, I sat up on the couch and gazed over at Ms. Gabriel.

"I already feel so much better," I stumbled over my words sleepily, the visions from the chakra balancing already fading into the background.

Chapter Fourteen

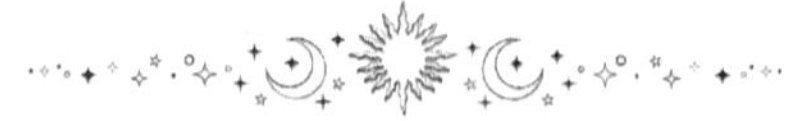

"**Y**ou need more money from me? Why? To buy yourself some more jewelry or what?" I yelled at my mother from the kitchen.

"You're nineteen now, and lucky for you, I still let you live here." She was sitting at the dining table and staring up at me. "So, you've got to help out."

Dante stood up from his recliner as Lola laid it on me. He moved to stand behind her, giving me a sour look.

"Oh, yeah. You know, I can't even afford tuition anymore because I keep giving you guys all my money." I reached into my purse and took out the cash Omar had given me earlier and set it on the table. "Here's fifty dollars. I'm leaving."

I stomped over to my room and started stuffing clothes, makeup, and hair products in a duffel bag. I flung my bag over my shoulder and stormed out of the house. The door slammed behind me.

After thirty minutes of walking under that brutal Florida sun, I arrived at a strip mall and sat down to text Omar. I found an old pack of cigarettes in my purse along with a lighter. Sitting on the edge of the curb, I lit one up and took a deep inhale. After each puff, I turned the burning side toward me and stared as the fine strips of tobacco glowed bright orange and then withered into smoke.

He called me back after about thirty minutes.

"Hey."

"Hi, what's going on?"

"I need somewhere to stay. I just left my house for good."

"Really? Well, now's not a good time. Go to a friend's house and hang out for a little while, and I'll text you when I'm free."

Luckily, Nikki was still in town visiting, and she came to pick me up after just a few minutes. That night we stayed up drinking, smoking, and laughing at everything. I didn't know what time we went to bed, but when I woke up around 10 a.m., my heart jumped when I saw Omar's missed text. It was time-stamped 4:13 a.m. What was he doing up until four in the morning?

I called him.

"What are you doing?" he asked.

"About to have breakfast here at Nikki's."

"Ok, I'll swing by to pick you up in a bit."

He brought me to his house. When we were settled and sitting comfortably on his couch with his arm around my shoulder he told me, "I want you to live here with me. You don't have to go home."

I released a deep, unsteady breath.

"Thanks, nene. Te quiero," I pressed my hand on his chest and curled farther into his arms.

He turned his head toward mine, and we locked in a kiss.

Later that evening, after I'd cooked a heavenly meal of rice, beans and grilled chicken, Omar got up and grabbed his keys and wallet.

"Where are you going?" I asked.

"Cariño, I've got to go take care of some things. You just relax here—in your new home." He came and planted a kiss on my cheek. I picked up the dishes and occupied myself with the cleaning. Still, thoughts began to enter my mind about some other woman he could be rushing off to see in the night, but I shoved them down.

Instead, I thought more about the dreams I kept having. I puzzled over why they hadn't stopped since I'd opened my chakras, and I wondered if Nikki's mom was right. What if I *could* do what she called precognition? Why were my dreams always so scary? And what was the fire all about?

My thoughts stayed with Ms. Gabriel, and I remembered that during our chakra session, she'd also shown me how to meditate. She explained that mediation during my waking life would help me control my mind better in my dreams.

After I finished washing the dishes, I noticed that unlike my parents' home, where the sound of the TV was always blaring in the background, here I couldn't hear anything but soothing silence. I made myself a cup of hot chamomile tea. As I was walking toward the bedroom, I felt drawn to the sliding glass doors leading to the backyard.

I slid the doors open to reveal a tropical garden sprawling with ferns, red ginger and palm trees. The light, cool breeze shuffling the leaves welcomed me as I stepped out onto the wooden patio and sat in an oversized wicker chair.

This was where I began my first solo meditation.

During the meditation, I felt a fierce pull from my core. I almost lost my balance on the chair and fell forward. The pull was followed by a bright light that glowed within my mind's eye. It showed the same crimson gate from the jaguar dream and the same dark-haired man standing underneath with that stone-cold look in his eyes. His hand was held out in front of him, and a flame burned bright from the inside. His lips parted, and he spoke words I couldn't understand. Slowly, flames licked around his entire body until he was fully consumed by them and disappeared.

Chapter Fifteen

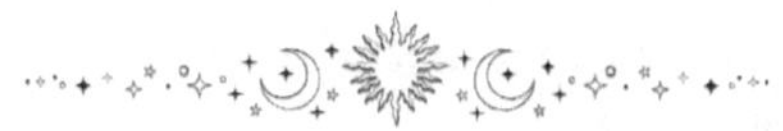

According to Omar, I didn't need to work, because he took care of all the bills. After all, he was an entrepreneur with a flexible and unpredictable schedule.

I looked out the window, shaken by the man who kept appearing in my dreams and meditations. I tried to focus instead on the branch of a tree shifting lightly in the wind.

I returned my gaze to Omar lying next to me in the bed. My eyes raked along his bare chest; the curves of his defined muscles glistened in the morning light. My core pulsed and ached with the memories of our intimacy. I swept my hand across his steel-cut abs. *I wonder if he's ready for another round.*

When I raised my eyes to meet his he said to me, "Let's get married."

I started to laugh. "Are you for real?"

"Yeah. Let's do it."

"Oh wow, you are serious." I lifted my head from the pillow and shifted my weight unto my elbow. His black eyes were unflinching. "Well, since you're being so romantic, fine. I'll marry you."

"Let's do it now. Let's go to the courthouse."

"Wait a minute. You mean just go and have them do it there, with no ceremony, no family, or friends? You mean, don't tell anyone?"

"Exactly. Just me and you. No one else matters anyway." He stood up in front of me, exposing his lean, muscular torso. He took a deep breath that lifted his chest ever so slightly.

This had the potential to piss a whole lot of people off. The girls who were still after Omar. Elio. My parents. Those who refused to believe he was really into me. They all might just think I was crazier than they'd even thought.

Or perhaps no one would think of me at all, because none of those people really cared about me anyway. Right now, all I had was Omar. I could become his wife and completely disappear from my previous life. Sounded pretty good to me. Nothing would make me happier.

"You think they'll be able to do it today?" I asked.

"I think so. Let's try."

"Ok, let's do it." I gave him a big smile that met my eyes.

We headed to the courthouse. I wore a short-sleeved beige sundress with light makeup, my dark hair down and loose and curled at the ends. He wore a beige button-down shirt that complemented his skin tone with designer khaki pants and brown Cole Haan shoes. We filled out some paperwork and were given a number.

As we settled in our two plastic chairs in the waiting area, I looked around the room. There were at least four other brides besides me. A few were dressed in white, carrying flower bouquets, with family and friends around. There was another young couple wearing jeans and T-shirts, laughing and holding hands, with what looked like good friends surrounding them.

Sitting next to Omar now, I saw him rubbing his hands together and not saying much at all. Was he nervous?

"I can't believe we're doing this." I rubbed my hands against my thighs with my shoulders perched up.

"Yeah, we are," he replied in a cool tone that I couldn't read but desperately wanted to.

I guess I was looking for excitement, happiness, something. I knew it was hard for a guy like him to show emotions, but at this point, I couldn't read him at all. I decided to throw a card on the table.

"I can't wait to be your wife," I hugged his muscular arm tightly, resting my cheek against his shoulder.

He brushed me off as he got up, walked to the counter, and spoke to the clerk.

When he returned, he said, "I think it'll be another fifteen to thirty minutes."

Why was he acting like we were at a bank and not our wedding? Well, it was probably better this way—much less complicated, I told myself.

It was our turn. The clerk called us to the counter and began the process. We signed some more paperwork, and the clerk asked us if we would take each other as lawfully-wedded wife and husband. When all that was done, the clerk turned to me and said, "You may now exchange rings."

My heart dropped when I realized we didn't have any. Then I looked up into his ebony eyes, and all my insecurity washed away. I wasn't going to let a silly detail like rings ruin the magic of today.

We both shrugged at the clerk, and she went on to say, "Well, that's ok. I pronounce you man and wife."

"May I kiss the bride?" He looked directly at me.

"If you want to," the clerk replied, uninterested.

Omar's lips caressed mine, and I felt like I would melt right then and there. He wrapped his arm tightly around my waist and pulled me closer. The clerk let out a soft cough. We ignored her.

Immediately after leaving, we headed to Omar's favorite restaurant in South Beach. The Mediterranean food was always fresh, delicious, and creatively served. It was booked months out but Omar knew the owner. Locals came for the great food and lively music; tourists came for the celebrity sightings. After today I was worried my cheeks would be permanently flushed, but my heart felt light as a feather.

This marriage—I believed it was mine. I thought I could start a new life with Omar. The thing was, I really thought I was free.

Omar took his time ordering. When the waiter approached the table, Omar said, "Bring us your best bottle of pinot grigio. We're celebrating."

The waiter obliged.

Then he laughed heartily when I said, "I bet the clerk wanted to watch us have sex later tonight."

"I don't know about the clerk, but I can't wait to watch myself."

I flushed with excitement as I realized we were officially husband and wife.

After the food arrived and we devoured each bite, I asked him, "So, my husband, how was your food?"

"It was delicious, my wife. How was yours?"

I licked my lips slowly after having our dessert, then said, "You want to know what this day tastes like? Just like candy."

Chapter Sixteen

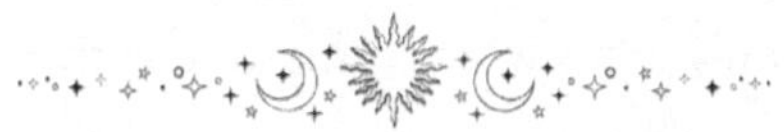

Once home, he reached for my arm as we entered the doorway, stopping me. He pulled me to him, reaching one hand up to my neck and held my face in his hand. His lips were a warm breath away from my neck, making me tingle everywhere in anticipation of his next touch. He slowly moved his face up until his eyes and lips met mine. He didn't kiss me, just held his lips a heartbeat away and whispered through his teeth, "You are mine now."

Although this excited me, and it was what I'd thought I wanted, it felt dangerous now. There with his hand grasping almost too tightly around my neck, I was completely overpowered by his strong hold. I was unable to move, even if I wanted to. With all my impulsiveness in running off and marrying him, I still didn't want to be his in the way it felt like he meant it now.

I looked at him and didn't speak. I didn't move. But if he could read my eyes, he would know I was beginning to question everything.

He spoke again. "Tell me you're mine. I need to hear you say it."

So much was uncertain. I was being forced to say something that a part of me didn't agree with. Although I had just married him, in this very moment, I felt powerless. So, I said it anyway. "I'm yours."

What I wanted this to mean was that he would take care of me. Keep me safe, give me a home, a new life away from my old influences—a life with new, better things. If that was what it meant to be his, I would be willing. Yet that wasn't how this felt. This felt like I couldn't breathe.

He started kissing me, very slowly at first. Then his muscles tensed, and he started putting more pressure on me. He moved his hands down from my neck to my waistline.

A heat rose from my center, and a delicious charge thrummed against my flesh.

He picked me up, and I eagerly wrapped my arms and legs around his strong back. He carried me like this to the kitchen counter where he pushed against me. I reciprocated by caressing his face and moving my hands down his hard chest and stomach to the front of his pants where I felt his erection pushing tightly against the fabric.

Hands clawed at my back as he pulled me closer, then released me slowly. "Walk over to the couch and bend over."

I walked slowly backward to the couch as heat pooled at the apex of my legs. I allowed myself to feel the sensuality of the moment and swayed my hips as I walked, looking alluringly at him as I did. Maybe all that stuff about being his in some kind of possessive, controlling way was all part of this game he was playing. I could play, too.

Turning over on the couch, bending my hips and looking at him over my shoulder, "Is this what you want?"

The way he was acting, I wasn't sure if my confidence would get him upset or make him want me more. Maybe it did a little of both.

He came over to me and yanked up the back of my dress. I wanted him to slow down, to stretch out this moment of anticipation, but he obviously didn't. He pulled down my white lace panties in less than a second. In a moment, I felt the length of him inside me, and a loud moan escaped my throat. He placed his hand firmly on my lower back, then let out a low growl of his own. He rocked back and forth, harder and faster with raw desire.

We moved around to the front of the couch, and when I searched his eyes, they had turned cold.

An icy chill shot through my veins. When he finished, he collapsed on top of me without a word. I felt small under him. Something had changed, and I didn't like it.

Soon we returned to our bedroom for the night, and in my sleep, the zodiac shadows returned.

It was daylight, and I was outside in a large, open field. There were the sounds of aircraft above, of people talking and bustling about, but I couldn't see anything except grass for miles. This would have otherwise been pleasant, if not for all the noise that just didn't belong in this scenery.

Then I saw another gate appear faintly in the distance. It was half the size of the Aries gate I'd kept seeing; instead, it was a deep green and covered with carvings of men and women in ancient garments surrounded by flowers. It was breathtaking. A single symbol was carved into the top of the archway, and I quickly recognized it as a bull. Taurus.

I looked beyond the gate and there was movement. People, strolling by. Unfamiliar shapes and sounds that seemed to exist just beyond the green arch, and something was not right. I had to leave. So, I started to lift off the ground and get into the air.

I had been flying in my dreams regularly. It was an easy thing to do, but this time I couldn't take flight. I was planted in place by a grab at my hand. When I turned around, I saw it was Omar. He was holding me down.

"Let go, I want to fly."

But he didn't answer, instead grabbing me tighter. After struggling and squirming, eventually I broke free of his grasp. As I flew higher into the sky, I kept looking at him, wondering if he could fly, too, if he could chase after me. Wondering if I was free.

That was when I heard the whispers again. As I heard the insistent sound, I looked up to see the now too-familiar vague and formless Shadow lift from my flesh while it simultaneously approached rapidly from the distance. The Shadow from within me joined together with the Shadow that approached. It was so perfectly uniform in its movement, full of mist and smoke, with a boundless darkness that filled the sky with night and covered the field. The indefinite mass barreled toward me, faster than ever before, like a herd of thousands of black jaguars pounding the ground as they ran toward me.

I floated higher in the only area of the field not completely engulfed in the ripples of black. My senses now awake, my nerves keenly in control, I felt a pervasive heaviness like suffocation. I tried to get away, but then I remembered Omar down below. I had to save him!

I dove quickly, but as I got within a few feet of him, I noticed his eyes were empty, like he was in a trance. He was not my Omar.

This imposter grasped at me until he'd pinned my arms, and I couldn't move.

"Let me go!" I yelled, fighting.

"You must be still. You must listen," the not-Omar answered.

His voice sounded of a multitude of beings speaking as one, something I had heard before, the first time the Shadow ever spoke to me.

Trembling, I stopped fighting him. I don't think I had ever been more afraid. At this point, I couldn't muster even a word, and the once-loud space fell completely silent except for an indistinct murmur at the edge of the dark, wild abyss that encroached upon us.

I dared to gaze behind the figure of not-Omar.

"This fantasy you are living in now will end soon for the rest of your life to begin. You must cross the gate." I shook my head, lost in confusion. Behind him the wall of darkness stopped and became still within just a few feet, surrounding us in a tight circle. With convulsive movements, various shapes and forms moved almost as one. Looking closer, I realized that these shapes were moving individually.

"Look within. The more you look, the more you will see," the thousand voices said in a whisper from not-Omar's lips.

I began to say, "I don't want to see," but I stopped myself mid-sentence when I caught sight of my Omar inside the black mist. He was being arrested. I wanted to yell out, to stop it from happening, but I didn't. Curious, I stood still and observed. I remembered the meditations and intentionally noticed my breathing—once frantic, it had begun to slow. I noticed my heart—once pounding quickly, it was becoming calm. And I noticed my mind—once locked in fear of this Shadow and what it would do to me, and now I was beginning to trust I would survive.

That night after I awoke from the nightmare, I was covered in sweat. I looked around the bed and noticed that Omar wasn't there. I hoped he hadn't heard me yelling in my sleep like Nikki used to. It was too early in our marriage to freak him out with my crazy dreams.

I got up for a cup of water and looked around the house. His keys were gone. I took out my notebook from the nightstand and wrote down the dream before I tried to go back to sleep. As I did, my mind turned to Omar. I began to wonder if I really knew who I'd married.

CHAPTER SEVENTEEN

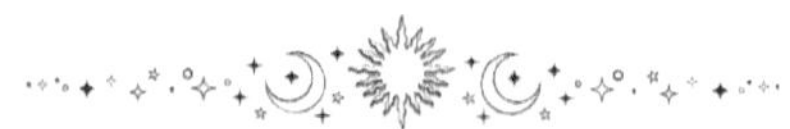

A few months later, I went back to the club where Omar worked as a DJ. I hadn't been in a while because he didn't want me there. But tonight, I was completely sick of staying home alone and needed some excitement.

I went with Olga, and we danced for a while before I saw Elio sitting in the VIP room with a girl on his lap. His gaze turned to meet mine just before I could avoid him. I thought I saw his expression brighten just a bit when he saw me. Maybe I was wrong.

Olga left me just then to chat with some guy, and then I saw Angel. He brought me to the bar and had the bartender pour me a drink.

"Tell me, Sashita, how are you?" he asked.

"I'm good. Especially now since Omar and I got married," I answered with the smile of a happy new bride.

Well, he killed my happy mood.

Angel's face dropped and his light demeanor completely shifted. He grabbed my shoulder and pulled me close enough to speak directly in my ear. "*Niña*, I'm only telling you this because you're my cousin. If you were anyone else, I wouldn't care less who Omar married. It's not my business. But listen, because I'm only going to say this once. Watch out."

My throat tightened.

"Watch out for what?" I asked as my shoulders and back tensed. I could do whatever I wanted; who was Angel to warn me about my husband?

"Watch out for yourself. I know you don't have anyone looking out for you, ok? And I know I'm not that person either. But what I can tell you is you don't want to get mixed up with the cartel. Plus, everyone knows you grew up around mafia. What if the cartel is playing you?"

"It's not like that." I shifted my gaze away from him and looked around the room, no longer interested in his presence.

Really, I was done with this whole conversation. I mean, I knew Omar was Sangre, and it didn't matter. Mafia didn't give a shit about me anymore, so he was fair game in my eyes. He loved me; I was sure of it. And more than that, he was protecting me by never telling me anything about his work. For all I knew, he ran an import and export business out of the Port of Miami. I didn't ask for specifics.

But what my cousin said stuck with me, because truth be told, Omar did act kind of shady sometimes. My face flushed with frustration that I hadn't seen all this before.

I left the club just then, my mood sour.

I wouldn't mention my conversation with Angel to Omar, but when we were having lunch the next day, I told him all about my dream.

"But, mi amor, you have to be careful. It was a wicked dream, and I don't want anything to happen to you."

He just laughed it off. "You don't have anything to worry about, ok? Everything is fine."

I smiled and gave him a little nod. I wanted to believe him.

Later that same day I got a text from Elio. *Married? Omar? WTF Sasha.*

My heart raced. It was the first time he'd reached out to me since the arrest. Angel must have told him.

Yes, married.

You'll regret it.

I already do, I thought and shook it off. Was he threatening me? My heart pounded loud in my chest.

He takes care of me, I texted.

Elio never wrote back.

On Saturday, around eight in the evening, a few of Omar's friends came over. Shawn strutted over to me with a wide grin and gave me a kiss on the cheek. He then went to the fridge and grabbed a beer.

Excited to have company and chat for a while, I took a glass from the cabinet and was pulling a bottle of wine from the wine fridge when Omar turned to me, "Baby, why don't you go to bed? Us guys want to hang out for a while."

Acid laced my mouth. My lips pursed, and I was about to protest when I saw that look. That stern, dull look that warned he had little tolerance for disagreement. The look that he'd given me right before he grabbed me by the wrist and shoved me against the wall when I made a snide comment. The look that came as he would wrap his hand around my neck and squeeze whenever I told him I wanted to see a girlfriend or go visit my parents. The look that was followed with gifts and flowers, with sweet caresses and apologies, as long as I played by his rules every time.

In an instant, that look made me feel like I was eight years old.

"Yes... Yes, of course," I mumbled as I returned the wine glass to its place on the shelf.

This was fine. *Everything was fine.* I had plenty to do in my room. Omar had taken me shopping for new makeup and clothes that still had the tags on. Well, at least I could try all those new clothes on, and even better, I could read a book and meditate.

I found that I loved to meditate. As soon as I started making meditation a habit, I found I would crave tea after each session. When I asked Nikki's mother about this, she explained that meditation aligned your body with your mind, and the needs of your body would be more clearly expressed. Apparently, my body needed chamomile tea with orange and spice.

After entertaining myself in the room for a while, I began to get stir-crazy.

I am not a child, I told myself.

He couldn't just keep telling me what to do and keep me from doing the things I wanted. I could do what I felt like. Who did he think he was, anyway?

The room started to feel small, like the walls were shrinking in. The air felt heavy and hot. Determined to show him just how strong and independent I could be, I went out to the kitchen to make myself a cup of tea.

When I walked in, I saw two of his friends at the table hanging out while Omar was doing something at the stove. I walked toward the stove to heat the teapot when Shawn saw me and got up from the table.

He stepped in between Omar and me. "Hey, what are you doing up?"

Omar looked over at me from behind his friend.

"I just came to get a cup of tea," I answered, annoyed I was being asked questions like this in my own house.

"Baby, baby... I'll bring you some tea, ok? Just go back to bed." Omar seemed surprised and clearly annoyed.

I turned and stomped off, slamming the door behind me. Was he cooking for the guys but not for me? The smell of cooked food was absent from the kitchen entirely. It was strange how Shawn was so quick to block my view. Something was obviously up with these guys.

Chapter Eighteen

I awoke that night to Omar's arms reaching for me under the sheets. His hands were full of lust as he moved them gently up and down, and my waist moved to his rhythm. Even when I was upset with him, my body would betray me to his touch. When I turned to face him, he reached his hand to my jaw, and sleepily I opened my eyes to his two deep dark pools. He kissed me gently, and I returned the kiss as I felt the pressure of his body weight pushing down on mine.

He lifted his lips from our kiss and whispered, "Never, ever come out of your room after I tell you to go to bed. You understand? Never disrespect me again."

My eyes opened wide at his demand, and I saw that look once again. He held my face with a grip on the verge of turning painful. The pressure of his body on mine intimidated me further. I knew it would be futile to argue with him now, even though I disagreed with him completely.

"Ok... ok, baby, of course. I would never disrespect you," I replied in the most sultry, submissive voice I could muster.

"Say it again."

"I will never disrespect you. I love you," I repeated, now with my voice serious and intent.

Then he pulled aside my black lace panties, and I felt him inside me. This was his way of making sure the message was clear. Wrapped in my passion for him, my fear of him, and even my fear of what my life would be like without him, I succumbed once again.

It went on like this for a while, where the guys would come over and he would tell me to go to bed and I would obey. And yet much of the time he just wouldn't be around, and I was left for days and nights simply alone.

I asked him about it one day.

"Nah baby, there's nothing going on, all right?" he assured me. "You have got to chill."

One afternoon, I was home alone folding the laundry when the phone rang. I picked it up and heard the automated message, "You have an inmate calling collect from the Miami-Dade County Pre-Trial Detention Center. Do you accept the charges?"

My heart sickened in an instant. "Yes."

"Hi, baby, it's Omar. Look, I've been arrested, and there are some pretty extensive charges on me."

"What are you talking about? Are you ok? What happened? I don't understand." My mind stirred, and a thousand thoughts rushed to my brain at once. Thoughts filled with anger, frustration and fear of what was going to happen now.

"Calm down. Everything is going to be fine. Listen, they have Shawn here, too. He's calling a lawyer for us both."

I took a deep, stilling breath. What the fuck do you mean, calm down. "What did you get arrested for?"

"Drug trafficking, possession of an unregistered firearm and aggravated assault," he replied.

I gasped.

"You know my hustle. Don't act surprised. Now, I gotta go. I'm going to try to call you again soon, but I'm not sure when. The lawyer might be in touch before I can."

"Wait, when are you getting out? How am I going to pay the bills? I can't even buy groceries!" I yelled in desperation.

"I need you to be strong, baby. You got this. I love you," he answered more gently than I would have expected.

His lawyer stopped by the apartment a week later. The place was a mess, as was I, wearing one of Omar's T-shirts that had a mysterious yellow food spilled on the front and a pair of sweatpants. I wasn't expecting anyone and had been too ashamed to tell anyone what was going on. I rushed to pick up the cushions and make the place seem presentable before opening the door.

The lawyer looked like a thug in a suit. After he entered, we sat at the kitchen table and he explained Omar's situation. "He's looking at a fifteen-year sentence, and if I can get the charges reduced, it may be that he serves five of the fifteen. He could potentially get out on parole even sooner if he plays his cards right. They want some information from him that he's not willing to share, so he's making this harder than it needs to be. Maybe you can talk to him?"

"Oh no, I don't think so," I replied. "When Omar gets something in his head, that's it. There's nothing you can do."

"Fine." His eyes narrowed in annoyance. "Now we need to talk about my fees. He told me you would pay the retainer."

My eyebrows furrowed, and I shook my head. It took me a moment to process what he was saying. My temperature was rising and my face started feeling flush. "Wait, what? I can't even afford to pay for rent. How can I pay your retainer?"

At first, I thought a look of concern showed in his eyes, but he was quick to snap out of it. "Look, Shawn already paid me part of my retainer. That was enough to get started, but to see their cases through, I need the rest. Have you searched the house? He might have some cash stashed somewhere. You better get to finding it before someone else does." He grunted as he moved his thumb and index finger up and down the lining of his jacket while scanning the room for I don't know what.

Of course, I had searched the house for a hidden stash. It'd been the first thing I'd done. I had been eating mustard out of the container because I literally had no money for food.

My stomach growled just then. Tears began to burn the bottoms of my eyes, but I wouldn't let a single drop spill down my cheek. I suddenly realized I had to really face this thing.

My despair was obviously making the lawyer uncomfortable because he stood up and scooted his chair back under the table. "Listen, here's my card. Omar owes me twenty-five thousand dollars for his portion. Call me when you have it. Either way, I'll be by next week to collect."

I had been walking around in a daze for days—totally lost, depressed that my world was caving in all around me, confused as to what to do next. But that guy was intimidating, and I didn't want to be here when he came back.

I needed money, fast.

I looked for work and quickly found a job as a receptionist at a nearby hair salon. The first day at work was someone's birthday, so there was cake to be shared, and I helped myself to three slices. Things were looking up.

Chapter Nineteen

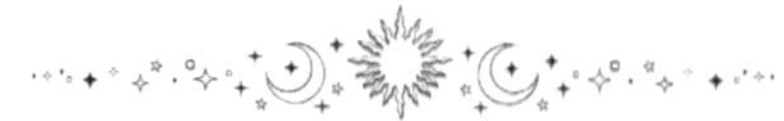

Finally, after days of waiting, Omar contacted me to give me the instructions for a visit at the jail. I made sure to dress the part. I wore a deep-burgundy long-sleeved blouse with a matching cotton pencil skirt and black booties. Somehow, the deep red color comforted me.

When I walked into the waiting room, the coolness of the yellow tile walls matched the nausea rising within me as the severity of the entire situation began to settle in. After waiting over an hour among scrambling children, girlfriends and dead-faced parents, I was told to go in and have a seat at the partition window. Omar was already there, and as I saw him sitting behind that partition, he reminded me of a mouse behind the glass at the pet store.

His beard was growing in a terrible way, his hair looked like it had not been combed for days and his eyes were bloodshot. A little too bloodshot. Despite all of this, he still brought up in me a heat that rose from my sacral to my heart chakra. I smiled to myself, as in that moment I realized how much better I was at identifying my chakras with all that meditating I was doing.

"Hey, love." He returned my smile with a smooth smile of his own as I picked up the phone.

I couldn't help but notice that his shadow was exceptionally pronounced for the lighting indoors, and I would be damned if I didn't see it swirling about with its own independent movements as if it were alive. In fact, this whole pitiful place seemed alive with darkness and fury.

"Hey, baby, how are you doing?" I asked.

"Good, shorty. Nothing to worry about. This will all be over soon."

"You think so? The lawyer came by. He didn't make it sound like anything would be over soon. He told me you owe him twenty-five thousand dollars."

"I got it covered." His smooth smile had completely disappeared.

"Ok, so tell me what I'm supposed to do now? I can't afford food. The bills are piling up. I don't know what to do."

He shifted in his chair, moving the receiver up and down as he did. "Don't tell me you have it hard, ok? Don't give me all these problems. I have it hard in here. I'm the one who's behind bars. You're free! You get to do whatever you want. I'm so sick of hearing your complaints, you mafia *bitch*!" He slammed the phone receiver on the glass.

A guard came over and stood behind him while I stared, stunned into silence. Omar may have been controlling and aggressive with me before, but he'd never called me *that*. He mumbled something to the guard that I couldn't understand, then picked up the phone again.

I spoke before he could. "'Mafia bitch?' Well at least this mafia bitch is free!" I growled tauntingly as a new kind of rage boiled deep within me.

I wanted to dig my claws into his eyes and scratch them out. I felt a prickly sting at the back of my neck and had the urge to rip into him with my teeth. My palms suddenly surged with heat, and I dropped the receiver abruptly thinking it was coming from there.

Omar looked at me with that familiar hateful stare I'd denied myself from noticing before.

This dipshit never loved me.

The guard motioned for him to hang up, and he was escorted out of the room. I was left sitting there alone, and it took all of my mental strength to keep from trying to get at him. It was like I knew I could tear down the glass and tear into him in a heartbeat. But that must have just been my anger getting away from me. Instead of making more of a scene, I focused on the one thing he was right about.

I was free, and I could do whatever I wanted.

When I arrived home, there was a letter taped to the door: an eviction notice. We were given thirty days to vacate the premises. There was a contact listed on the letter, so I called to see if I could buy some time. They told me I was already on borrowed time, and that Omar hadn't paid the rent in three months. Well, surprise, surprise. My day just kept getting better.

I opened the door and looked around the empty apartment. Anything of value had been pawned days before, thanks to my blossoming relationship with the pawn store. It was now almost completely bare with just a few dining stools, a white leather sofa and a chair. I walked into the bedroom closet which only had about four shirts and pants on the hangers and a few items folded on the shelves.

The reality was that I wasn't even considering fighting for Omar's freedom. But I had nowhere to turn. I hadn't spoken to my family or friends in months. I dropped to my knees on the gray closet carpet.

The only person I could think of right now was my aunt Lily and how badly I wanted to be wrapped up in her arms as she told me the stories of the zodiac. She'd shared many stories from different cultures, like the Chinese, Indian, Mayan and Greek zodiac myths.

As I sat there, hiding in the barren closet, I remembered the Capricorn story of the sea-goat Pricus who could manipulate time. Pricus, being the father of a race of intelligent sea-goats that could speak, couldn't keep his children from going to shore and changing into the goats we knew today. This bothered him very much, so he turned back time and forbade them from going on land.

But no matter how many times he tried, they would live out this destiny. He finally realized he couldn't keep them from becoming these mindless land-based creatures and decided to stop trying. This made Pricus very upset because his family left him all alone in the ocean. In his loneliness, he begged the god of time, Chronos, to allow him to die. Chronos instead decided to let him live out his immortality in the sky as the constellation Capricorn, watching his children from above.

How I wanted to turn back time right now. I wanted to be back in school, Nikki to still live in Miami and Elio to not have ghosted me. But just like the story goes, no matter how much I tried to turn back time, I would probably end up exactly where I was right now. Pathetic, alone and praying to my dead aunt in a closet that was no longer mine.

The stars write the path, Lily would always say.

I miss you so much, Lily. I'm so lost. I don't know what else to do. Are you there, listening? I don't know who I am or what is right. I just know this is all wrong.

I closed my eyes and cried. I didn't expect a response, but it was all I had. I remembered then the vision of Omar being arrested. I saw a spark ignite deep within my soul, and I knew there was more in this world for me.

I sat there quietly in stillness, listening. The words from my dream returned to me.

In the calm after the tears, I heard my own voice inside my head say, *Tomorrow, when you wake up, find a way to file for divorce. You know you don't love him, and you never did. Call your parents, and ask them if you can move back in. You can get yourself out of this.*

As much as the thought of living with my parents again brought on shivers, I stood up and nodded to myself in that closed-in space. Now I knew what to do.

Chapter Twenty

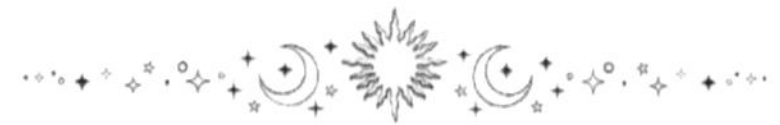

I carefully put on a light taupe lip gloss in the bathroom. After I checked myself, I said out loud to the girl I saw in the mirror, "You got this. It's almost over."

I walked down the hallway of wood-paneled walls and paisley carpets until I reached the waiting room. My lawyer stood up, and together we entered the judge's conference room. The room was tight, the table too big for the space. The chairs were oversized leather seats that also seemed to make everything in the room denser.

Michael, my lawyer, was in his early thirties and stood tall with dirty blond hair and gentle eyes. He was comforting to have next to me.

I'd forgiven him for not wanting to take the case at first. He'd turned it down when I'd told him I couldn't afford to pay him any more than $250. I'd found him through an ad in the newspaper that read, *Quick and Easy Divorce for $200*. When I called and explained the case, he told me it would be more involved than just filing papers. Then, when we met in person, I guessed he could see from my bloodshot eyes and ninety-five-pound, clammy, pale frame that I hadn't been lying about not having any money.

In the conference room, I waited patiently, not saying a word until the judge arrived. The judge walked in and greeted everyone. My shoulders dropped, and I exhaled slowly—this would be over soon.

"You are Sasha Moreno, the petitioner?" the judge said.

"Yes, Your Honor," I replied.

"Where is Omar Garcia?" the judge asked.

My throat tightened as soon as I heard the question.

"He's in jail, Your Honor," the lawyer answered.

Michael looked at me with a crease in his forehead and compassion in his eyes. The judge reviewed the motions and the signed divorce papers that had been served to Omar in jail.

"So the divorce is uncontested," the judge said. "This should be straightforward. Except, I do see you are in a great deal of debt. I order you both to split it fifty-fifty, and you are equally responsible for paying it."

"Thank you, Your Honor, but most of the debt is from credit cards in my name. What if he doesn't pay?"

The judge simply answered, "You'll have to figure that out."

After all the papers had been signed and we'd left the courtroom, I gave Michael a great big hug. I realized then that there were people willing to help other people when they were at their worst simply because it made them feel good.

I took in his nice suit, trim haircut and close shave, and for the first time, I realized how handsome he was. Then I wondered if the only way I could meet someone like him—someone well-educated with a career, financial stability and probably a wholesome upbringing—would be as a victim that needed representation. I considered this as I watched him walk toward his car on the busy sidewalk.

For some reason, I didn't want to say goodbye. I stood there staring at him. I wanted to learn. To ask him questions like, how could I start doing things right, like him? How could I start living a better life? I knew I still had a chance to turn things around, but I didn't know how.

When he turned to face me, I guess he saw the question in my eyes, because he said, "Now, don't go marrying any more drug dealers."

I answered, "Trust me, I won't."

He turned to leave me, then turned back. I saw his eyes light up with a bit of daring in them. "Do you mind if I ask what got him arrested?"

"Well, do you want the short or long version of the story? If you want the long version, you'll have to treat me to lunch, because I'm starving."

"Well, let's go, then. This should be interesting."

We sat down at the corner diner. I ordered a Coke, onion rings, steak with mushrooms, mashed potatoes and broccoli. He ordered a roast beef sandwich with extra mustard and fries.

"You going to eat all that?"

"Watch me," I answered. Before the food came, I told him what I knew. "I only know what I pieced together from the lawyer, police reports and my own suspicions." I took a deep breath. "Apparently, there was an undercover operation involving the DEA and the FBI. It seems they had been watching Omar for months. Somehow, he got involved with undercover agents who asked him and Shawn for a lot of cocaine and oxy. And Omar, of course, was all about the money.

"Ever since I moved in with him, he kept telling me our place was temporary. We even went with a realtor to check out a penthouse in one of the new buildings downtown. He also said he would buy me a new car, so I bet this was how he'd planned to pay for all the things he—I mean, we—wanted."

The waiter set two waters and two straws down in front of us. I took the paper off my straw and rolled it up with my fingers, needing to do something with my hands.

"They found an empty house in a nice neighborhood and picked it as their meeting point. I figured it was Omar who'd picked the place because he knows those areas well. He used to get hired to DJ at parties over there all the time. Anyway, after he sold the undercovers the drugs, they told him he was under arrest. When he tried to run, they shot the car tires out. He then lost his damn mind and took three shots at the police, injuring one of them."

The little paper from the straw was now the tiniest little ball that I wished I could squeeze even tighter.

The food was served, and the smell of grilled mushrooms and steak was intoxicating. As I ate, I completely forgot I was with Michael.

He snapped me out of it when he said, "You've been through a lot, Sasha. It seems like you've gotten through the worst of it now. You sound like you read those reports in detail."

"I found them interesting."

"Maybe that's something you could look into. Becoming an investigator. Maybe even a lawyer."

"You think so?" I looked down at my food then. "I dropped out of college when I married Omar. Not sure what I'm going to do with myself now."

Michael leaned back in the booth and I raised my eyes to meet his. "You could always join the military. You're what, eighteen? That's the perfect age. My brother joined right out of high school and became a mechanical engineer. He's pretty happy with it."

"How do I even do that?"

"I'll give you his number. You can call him, and I'm sure he'll be happy to explain it all to you."

After lunch, Michael got in his shiny sedan and drove off. I headed toward the bus station, not sure what to do next, but I had Michael's brother's number in my pocket, and at least that was something. I had been fighting for months to be free of Omar. It was my only goal.

Now that it was done, I had a new beginning. As I stared into space the entire bus-drive home, I knew I had to make leaving him behind worth it.

I arrived at my old bedroom that I had once wished to never see again. I wanted to celebrate but couldn't. I wanted to go tell someone—anyone—that it was all over. That I'd just done this incredibly hard thing. But there was no one to tell. My mother wasn't speaking to me; she barely let me back in the house. My father was just... himself. Nikki was living her best life in New York, without me. When I lay down that night and closed my eyes, I felt worthless.

Exhaustion washed over me, but as soon as I drifted off to sleep, I remembered the shadow.

Night after night, the zodiac shadows would visit, and I would run at the first sight of them. Ever since I'd decided to leave Omar, the nightmares had gotten worse. The Shadow would completely envelop me no matter how much I fought. It was overpowering.

It came from both inside and outside my body, and it was impossible to escape. Horrific scenes from inside the void would consume me, and I would be drenched in the agony of all the tortured souls within its depths. Still, there was an even deeper part of me that wanted the shadows to come. That was a part of me I couldn't understand.

At times, the visions were so gripping that I would wake up and rush into the bathtub of the hallway bathroom. As I waited inside, the dark would still come for me. It made a deafening howl in the middle of the night that no one heard but me.

My nails were chewed to stubs as I sat inside that bathtub, looking around and hearing the high-pitched whisper come closer every second. I lifted my hands to cover my ears and felt the sweat and oil on my hair make my skin itch. I searched the cracks around the door for signs it was close, but there was nothing there yet.

Bare feet slid on the scratched porcelain tub as I curled my knees into my arms, wrapped my hands together and held on tight. My forehead touching my knees, I waited for the midnight mist to come.

Chapter Twenty One

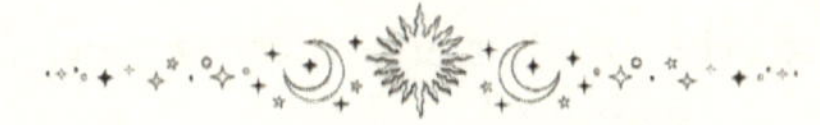

*S**tatic in my ears.*

> *Screams and whispers.*

Forces pulling.
Burns on my skin.
Drip.
Darkness all around. Tortured souls and howls.
Drip.
It comes in the night.
It lurks in the day.
It presses on my chest.
Drip. Drip. Drip.

I focused on the dripping faucet, listened to it. Paralyzed with fear, I struggled to move my arm from around my knees to touch the next drop of the water that dripped from the faucet. I thought only about this drop as the night's dark tormenter surrounded me. The cool water moistened my finger and was not afraid of the Shadow. The water didn't construct a thought about the destruction the dark wanted for me. It just went on dropping like there was no gallery of monsters here.

In the middle of the hurricane of wickedness surrounding me, I counted the drops as they fell. I was up to fifteen when the Shadow started to fade into the background. It slithered back and released its grip on my senses. This was the first time in weeks this had happened. Now I knew what to do. This was when I learned how to make it back off.

It still came every night, and instead of running for the bathtub, I found a constant to focus on. I always heard the darkness before it came, and that was when I began my new ritual. I would focus on one thing in my room that I could count until the Shadow settled.

Last night, I counted the blinds on my window. There were thirty-two. Another night, I counted the number of corners of every square or rectangle in the room. There were twenty-five.

If the Shadow wasn't gone by the time I finished counting, I used other tricks, like describing things. One night, I focused on my vanity. It had four drawers—three on the right and one on top of the open area where the chair slid in. It was a light-pink color with a large rectangular mirror with a matching frame mounted on top. Modern in design, it had no curves, only straight lines. Then the sound stopped, and the Shadow faded away.

Before I'd discovered counting things that night in the bathtub, I'd wondered if these zodiac shadows would ever stop. I wondered if anyone else saw it, but when I tried to bring it up, I just sounded crazy. I had stopped eating and weighed next to nothing. At one point, I'd given up trying to live with it. I swallowed a bottle of sleeping pills with half a bottle of Don Q rum to make it go away. The next morning, I'd opened my eyes to the harsh reality that I would face this thing another day.

After a few days of counting and describing, I began to sleep at night again, and when I did, my mind was filled with vivid lucid dreams. Dreams of a different life than I had now. Dreams where I met new people and flew to unimaginable places. Dreams where I had control of my life and in those dreams, I was powerful. I ran through grassy fields and forests. My bones and muscles were firm and strong, and my mind was clear and focused. In those dreams, I hunted.

One day, after watching a movie I was inspired by a scene where the main character spent all night studying. It occurred to me that there had to be some information on this thing. The next day I went to the library to research anything I could about these visions and dreams. As I entered the brown building with outdated furniture and breathed in the smell of humid wood in the air, I felt safe.

No miserable shadow screeching howls or dark creepy mist here. I wanted to stay forever.

I made myself comfortable on the hard oak library chair, set down a stack of books on the matching shiny oak table and began to take notes. I read about psychology, light, sound and perception. I hoped I would find clues about myself and what was happening to me.

I learned that the way the human eye processed light is a psychological phenomenon, and much of it is still unknown. There are areas of the electromagnetic spectrum invisible to the average human, just like there are sound frequencies the average ear cannot hear. Research even showed that some humans have ultrasonic hearing. They can perceive higher frequency sounds than what is ordinarily audible.

After about four hours sitting in that chair, I opened myself to the tiniest possibility that I was perceiving the world differently. That I saw parts of the electromagnetic spectrum that others didn't. That I heard sounds that the normal human ear couldn't hear. This presented a new realm of possibility. The smallest chance of hope that there was something more to my night terrors, something that meant I was not psychotic. And that if I could accept this, then I could adapt. I could find a way to compensate and still live a normal life. This information could help me stay grounded while I tried to normalize my crazy.

I remembered what I learned in the bathtub, how counting and describing things helped ease the fright away. Even still, the darkness was relentless in its return. I began to retake some control of my mind and when I did, I was able to fight harder to escape the reach of the shadows. I knew it wanted something from me. I knew it was a part of me. But I had no clue what to do.

I would then conjure up a memory of a faraway place I'd visited that the Shadow didn't know, like the fruit farm in Homestead that my mother once took us to as a child, or my aunt's house in Puerto Rico that I visited a few times over summers. The dark mist couldn't reach me there, but I had to be lucid enough in the dream to shape my reality.

One place I never wanted the shadow to know about was my aunt Lily's house in Villalba, Puerto Rico. You could see the mountains from the balconies, spreading out across the horizon with acres of tropical trees, lakes, and farmland.

Blooming fuchsia bougainvilleas, red flamboyant trees, and hibiscus flowers decorated the lush green landscape, and unlike the lower altitudes, in Villalba the air was always fresh and cool. They had goats, cows, horses and other livestock on her fifty-plus acres, and during one of the few summers I visited, I found an abandoned goat shed. It was near the main property but far enough away for me to find some refuge.

One day, after deciding to escape the noise of the main house, I filled a backpack with a pillow, a blanket and some snacks and headed off to the goat shed. I sat inside, reading a book, eating alcapurrias, and after some time I fell asleep to the sound of coquis in the night.

When I returned to the main house the next morning, my mother and uncle interrogated me for hours. I didn't want them to know about my secret hideaway, so I lied and told them I climbed a tree by the lake. I had never felt safer than I did in that goat shed. This was the one safe place I had to protect from my broken reality.

From then on, I would go to my goat shed in my dreams. I reconstructed every corner, every stone, even my little drawing on the wooden panel by the entry. I carved my Aries ram sign right into the wood, next to my Mayan zodiac sign, the jaguar. I was at peace in that goat shed, and for now it would have to be enough. It wouldn't be easy, but I was determined to get a grip on my mind, if only from one moment to the other, by putting one foot in front of the other. Right now, in my life, any more than that would be too much.

As my Titi Lily would say, sometimes everything needs to get worse before it can get better. Little did I know the worst was yet to come.

Hey, it's me. Sasha.

This is just the beginning of my story and even though sometimes I want to smack that younger version of me across the face for all the dumbass decisions she made, I have to thank her. Now I can see she needed to go through all of that, to get me where I am today.

So, if you enjoyed this story, you should subscribe to R.C. Luna's newsletter for updates on her new books. Especially since there is so much to tell about my story in her next book, Zodiac Fate - Keep reading! The first chapter in that book is on the very next page. You would also do her a real solid if you left a review for Zodiac Shadows. It would help get the word out about these books, in a major way.

www.rcluna.com

Xoxo, Sasha

Zodiac Fate

Chapter 1

I saw and heard very strange things by my twentieth birthday. Like a now familiar wicked darkness that moved and shifted in corners, indefinite and undefined. It crept forward with a certain boldness, thicker and darker than ever before.

In these solemn years before my transformation I faintly remembered a conversation with my aunt where she explained I would meet someone to help me with all this. But she died before she could tell me that the shadows would cover the walls as they slithered toward me, accompanied by a dark mist that held the creatures of the underworld within them. *They had hands with claws that reached for me!*

I saw them, demons in the corner with feverish eyes piercing into me in the night. I always felt them there, hidden, among shadows. One had a long, reptilian tail that rattled on the body of a massive alligator with a snake's head.

But there were more. Decaying bodies with black rotted flesh and sharp, long gray teeth, bald heads and protruding bones. Some without eyes. Some without mouths. Some without ears.

The beasts of the shadows called me to them day and night. In my nightmares there would be a gate with a zodiac sign. But I always had to fight through the shadows to get to it. That's why I called this living nightmare the Zodiac Shadows.

The months went by, and the heavy darkness only got stronger with no sign of any relief. Slowly and without me knowing it, my mind began to slip from my grasp.

It got exponentially worse after I left my ex, the rising mafia king. I'd married him in a rush to get out of my parents' house, already driven half-mad by the shadows.

And not surprisingly, that didn't work out either. My pitiful life was back to where it had all begun. In my old room at my parent's house, staring at the same popcorn ceiling I had run away from.

I shuffled from the kitchen to my room, whenever absolutely necessary. My hair oily and unwashed, my clothes stained, and it seemed nothing was ever where I left it.

One day, I made the mistake of unlocking my door while my father was in the hallway. I would've avoided him, but I couldn't hear him out there. Sounds of this world were muffled by the screeching howls of another place. Another time. He grabbed me by the hair, shoved a mop and bucket into my hands, and pressed me up against the wall. My legs and body buckled as weak as a withered flower.

"I've been knocking at your door," he said. "Didn't you hear me? Clean this place up if you want to live here."

I slowly took the mop from him, nodding and not meeting his eyes.

The desperate Zodiac Shadows swirled everywhere. The demons were my company. With my head in such a state, it was hard to remember things. What was it my aunt used to say? *Oh yes. The stars write the path.*

Just as it did every night, the Shadow would swirl around me, whispering the thoughts I dared not think, filling me with the power of its fury. A power that was ripping me apart. Sleep would only make it worse. My nightmares were so real. So disturbing that I slept as little as possible.

Until I could fight it no longer. My eyelids heavy, the day weary upon me, I couldn't stop myself this time and fell asleep.

I was dreaming again. I stood in a busy shopping area in downtown Miami. This was where Nikki and I loved to shop for new sneakers! I searched for her, my best friend since I was six. I missed her so much since she'd moved to New York. I missed her so much I wouldn't call her because she left me all alone, and I couldn't bear to hear how happy she was in her new life.

I was lost without her.

A familiar agony washed over me every time I thought about it. But when I peered into our favorite shop, there she was, checking out a new pair of shoes.

I went right up to her, as I always did, and said, "Yo, nice kicks."

She turned to me and smiled her big, beautiful smile. It was her, nose ring and all.

"Let's get a bite to eat, Nikki. I'm hungry."

Instantly, we were sitting across from each other in my favorite bodega where they served the best Colombian arepas and coffee. I looked down, and the food was already there on my plate.

I went to take a bite of the arepa but stopped before it met my mouth. My bones froze when I saw the Shadow creep in from the windows and the door, its smoke rolling ever so gently with the mist and whispers that accompanied the darkness swirling in its dreadful chasm.

"Nikki, Nikki! We've got to go," I yelled, but Nikki went on telling me a story I couldn't even hear—all I heard were the high-pitched whispers.

The Shadow was inches away from her, so I got up, grabbed her hand, and pulled so we could run. But she was locked in place. Frozen. She seized my arm, and I looked into her eyes. All at once they turned pale red with a bright violet ring around her pupils. I tried to shake off the haze, but it was no use.

The Zodiac Shadows had me now.

"Sit down," the not-Nikki form growled at me.

A deep knowing stirred within me, and by command, I sat. Unable to do otherwise.

The form released its control of my mind and spoke in the most pretentious voice I'd ever heard. "Listen, because we don't have much time."

I nodded and listened, the background of the café crumbling and rebuilding into a patio by a river bend, the river black and murky. I shifted my gaze to the waves of the river, stirring and brimming. Large, dark shapes the size of humans swam just beneath the surface.

"First of all, this shadow you see around you is an infection, inside your mind," the not-Nikki said. "I can't explain now, it's all too complicated for the dream state. But I am here to tell you that you need to cross the Gate, and soon.

"Unfortunately for you, your shaman has been off the grid for a while, and your shaman is the only one who can help with your induction. Simply put, you need to find your shaman and cross the Gate, or you will lose yourself to the shadows." She paused for a moment, assessing me. My brows pinched and I looked at her in utter confusion.

She furrowed her brows and centered on me. "Basically, just get your shit together and figure out a way to control your mind until you find the missing shaman and we can get you into the Aries Academy. Do you understand me?"

I stared wide-eyed at the not-Nikki and nodded robotically, even though I wasn't understanding much of anything. This creature, or mist, or force of nature—whatever it was—was giving me advice? Now? After making me fucking crazy for months?

Her voice sounded centuries old, her shoulders relaxed, and her demeanor was elegant and poised, unlike the rowdy Nikki I'd always known.

"You're behind in your training, Nagual. There is normally a formal introduction to the twelve Zodiac houses by now." The form stared away as if some distant voice was calling it. It turned back to me and said, "Remember, control your fucking mind."

Just then, the smell of bacon and eggs overwhelmed me, and I heard my name being called from somewhere far away...

⸺ ⁘ ⸺

The shadows were only the beginning.

If you're ready for more in this rapidly expanding new world—where the stars do more than whisper Sasha's fate from the darkness, visit rcluna.com.

Read more in the...
Warrior Shifter Series

Acknowledgements

Becoming an independent author is a long, lonely journey, thank the stars that these people were in my life and helped me get here. I am SO grateful:

Manuel, my husband, who keeps telling me my books will be Netflix movies one day. This is the kind of support a self-deprecating debut writer like me truly needs. My children, for all the times I turned you away from my office and told you I had to work. I must thank my consultant of the stars, Nazly. And everyone that supports me so closely. Your belief in me pushes me further each day. Of course, I can't forget to mention that my editor, Shavonne, cover designer, Miblart and to Ramy, my mentor, for saying "write that Latina FMC!" You all are the foundation I needed to make this happen.

And I can't say enough about the support system I have around me. Those amazing friends that have been rooting me along every step of the way and have told me that it's ok to be completely crazy and follow my dreams. And my family in Puerto Rico that is always there for me: Titi Ana y Titi Marga. I feel supported and loved by all of you.

Love you all so much!

About the Author

R.C. Luna is a Puerto Rican author who writes for those of us who were told we were too much. For the wild, magical, passionate, and restless minds who crave stories pulsing with desire, complexity, hunger, and transformation. Her work blends dark fantasy, ancestral mythology, and real-life emotion into high-stakes tales that shimmer with stardust and shadow.

Luna believes magic is too big to be contained, too wild to be confined—and so are we. Her stories are soul-deep, fierce, and always aching to reveal what's been silenced. She writes for readers who are ready to see themselves on the page.

When she's not writing, she's chasing moonlight with her husband, plotting chaos with her daughters and dog, Rumi, or channeling stories that refuse to stay quiet.

Learn more at www.rcluna.com

Enter the shadows.

Here's where you can find more magic, updates, and behind-the-scenes content — follow me on my socials and join the newsletter on my website!

www.rcluna.com
TikTok @author_rcluna
Facebook @authorrcluna
Instagram @author_rcluna

R.C. LUNA
EDGY FANTASY & ROMANCE
www.rcluna.com

THE STORY OF THE BAT

Date ....

Name of Animal ....

1. Is it domesticated or wild?

2. Estimate it's length and height.

3. Study the head: the shape of the ears, how placed, are they movable? The color, size and position of the eyes, the form of the nose and its position, the shape of the mouth, what kind of teeth and for what are they fitted? The shape and use of the tongue, are there any whiskers or feelers about the mouth?

4. Are the legs long or short? How many toes on the front feet and hind feet? Are they armed with claws? Are the feet padded? Are the legs and feet fitted for running, leaping, creeping, grasping, or clinging? Is the tail long or short? What is its covering? What is its use? How is the animal covered? How does its covering protect it? What is its color above and below? Does it help the animal to hide from its enemies or is it ornamental?

5. On what does the animal feed? How does it gets its food? If it carries its food, how?

6. Does it live on or beneath the ground or in trees, or in water or elsewhere?

7. Does it live alone or with mate or in a herd or flock?

8. Is it active during the day or night?

9. Where is its home, how is it made and how is it kept? Is it for itself or for its young?

10. Are its movements quick and active, strong and bold, stealthy or shy? Does it walk, run, leap or dart?

11. Where and in what position does it sleep?

12. How does it play? How does it show anger, pleasure, fear?

13. Has it a voice, if so, describe its uses.

14. How does it keep clean?

15. How does it care for its young? Do both parents take part in this? How are the young fed, carried, kept clean, defended, protected and taught to care for themselves? Are the young ever punished, if so, how?

16. How does this animal escape from its enemies? How does it fight them?

17. How does it live through winter?

NOTES ON THE BLACK BEAR

The Black Bear

NOTES ON THE BLACK BEAR

Date ....

Name of Animal ....

1. Is it domesticated or wild?

2. Estimate it's length and height.

3. Study the head: the shape of the ears, how placed, are they movable? The color, size and position of the eyes, the form of the nose and its position, the shape of the mouth, what kind of teeth and for what are they fitted? The shape and use of the tongue, are there any whiskers or feelers about the mouth?

4. Are the legs long or short? How many toes on the front feet and hind feet? Are they armed with claws? Are the feet padded? Are the legs and feet fitted for running, leaping, creeping, grasping, or clinging? Is the tail long or short? What is its covering? What is its use? How is the animal covered? How does its covering protect it? What is its color above and below? Does it help the animal to hide from its enemies or is it ornamental?

5. On what does the animal feed? How does it gets its food? If it carries its food, how?

6. Does it live on or beneath the ground or in trees, or in water or elsewhere?

7. Does it live alone or with mate or in a herd or flock?

8. Is it active during the day or night?

9. Where is its home, how is it made and how is it kept? Is it for itself or for its young?

10. Are its movements quick and active, strong and bold, stealthy or shy? Does it walk, run, leap or dart?

11. Where and in what position does it sleep?

12. How does it play? How does it show anger, pleasure, fear?

13. Has it a voice, if so, describe its uses.

14. How does it keep clean?

15. How does it care for its young? Do both parents take part in this? How are the young fed, carried, kept clean, defended, protected and taught to care for themselves? Are the young ever punished, if so, how?

16. How does this animal escape from its enemies? How does it fight them?

17. How does it live through winter?

NOTES ON THE BOB-CAT

The Bob-Cat

THE STORY OF THE BOB-CAT

Date ....

Name of Animal ....

1. Is it domesticated or wild?

2. Estimate it's length and height.

3. Study the head: the shape of the ears, how placed, are they movable? The color, size and position of the eyes, the form of the nose and its position, the shape of the mouth, what kind of teeth and for what are they fitted? The shape and use of the tongue, are there any whiskers or feelers about the mouth?

4. Are the legs long or short? How many toes on the front feet and hind feet? Are they armed with claws? Are the feet padded? Are the legs and feet fitted for running, leaping, creeping, grasping, or clinging? Is the tail long or short? What is its covering? What is its use? How is the animal covered? How does its covering protect it? What is its color above and below? Does it help the animal to hide from its enemies or is it ornamental?

5. On what does the animal feed? How does it gets its food? If it carries its food, how?

6. Does it live on or beneath the ground or in trees, or in water or elsewhere?

7. Does it live alone or with mate or in a herd or flock?

8. Is it active during the day or night?

9. Where is its home, how is it made and how is it kept? Is it for itself or for its young?

10. Are its movements quick and active, strong and bold, stealthy or shy? Does it walk, run, leap or dart?

11. Where and in what position does it sleep?

12. How does it play? How does it show anger, pleasure, fear?

13. Has it a voice, if so, describe its uses.

14. How does it keep clean?

15. How does it care for its young? Do both parents take part in this? How are the young fed, carried, kept clean, defended, protected and taught to care for themselves? Are the young ever punished, if so, how?

16. How does this animal escape from its enemies? How does it fight them?

17. How does it live through winter?

NOTES ON THE CAMEL

The Camel

OUTLINE FOR STUDY OF AN ANIMAL

Date ....

Name of Animal ....

1. Is it domesticated or wild?

2. Estimate it's length and height.

3. Study the head: the shape of the ears, how placed, are they movable? The color, size and position of the eyes, the form of the nose and its position, the shape of the mouth, what kind of teeth and for what are they fitted? The shape and use of the tongue, are there any whiskers or feelers about the mouth?

4. Are the legs long or short? How many toes on the front feet and hind feet? Are they armed with claws? Are the feet padded? Are the legs and feet fitted for running, leaping, creeping, grasping, or clinging? Is the tail long or short? What is its covering? What is its use? How is the animal covered? How does its covering protect it? What is its color above and below? Does it help the animal to hide from its enemies or is it ornamental?

5. On what does the animal feed? How does it gets its food? If it carries its food, how?

6. Does it live on or beneath the ground or in trees, or in water or elsewhere?

7. Does it live alone or with mate or in a herd or flock?

8. Is it active during the day or night?

9. Where is its home, how is it made and how is it kept? Is it for itself or for its young?

10. Are its movements quick and active, strong and bold, stealthy or shy? Does it walk, run, leap or dart?

11. Where and in what position does it sleep?

12. How does it play? How does it show anger, pleasure, fear?

13. Has it a voice, if so, describe its uses.

14. How does it keep clean?

15. How does it care for its young? Do both parents take part in this? How are the young fed, carried, kept clean, defended, protected and taught to care for themselves? Are the young ever punished, if so, how?

16. How does this animal escape from its enemies? How does it fight them?

17. How does it live through winter?

28

NOTES ON THE CHIMPANZEE

The Chimpanzee

THE STORY OF THE CHIMPANZEE

OUTLINE FOR STUDY OF AN ANIMAL

Date ....

Name of Animal ....

1. Is it domesticated or wild?

2. Estimate it's length and height.

3. Study the head: the shape of the ears, how placed, are they movable? The color, size and position of the eyes, the form of the nose and its position, the shape of the mouth, what kind of teeth and for what are they fitted? The shape and use of the tongue, are there any whiskers or feelers about the mouth?

4. Are the legs long or short? How many toes on the front feet and hind feet? Are they armed with claws? Are the feet padded? Are the legs and feet fitted for running, leaping, creeping, grasping, or clinging? Is the tail long or short? What is its covering? What is its use? How is the animal covered? How does its covering protect it? What is its color above and below? Does it help the animal to hide from its enemies or is it ornamental?

5. On what does the animal feed? How does it gets its food? If it carries its food, how?

6. Does it live on or beneath the ground or in trees, or in water or elsewhere?

7. Does it live alone or with mate or in a herd or flock?

8. Is it active during the day or night?

9. Where is its home, how is it made and how is it kept? Is it for itself or for its young?

10. Are its movements quick and active, strong and bold, stealthy or shy? Does it walk, run, leap or dart?

11. Where and in what position does it sleep?

12. How does it play? How does it show anger, pleasure, fear?

13. Has it a voice, if so, describe its uses.

14. How does it keep clean?

15. How does it care for its young? Do both parents take part in this? How are the young fed, carried, kept clean, defended, protected and taught to care for themselves? Are the young ever punished, if so, how?

16. How does this animal escape from its enemies? How does it fight them?

17. How does it live through winter?

32

NOTES ON THE COUGAR

The Cougar

THE STORY OF THE COUGAR

Date ....

Name of Animal ....

1. Is it domesticated or wild?

2. Estimate it's length and height.

3. Study the head: the shape of the ears, how placed, are they movable? The color, size and position of the eyes, the form of the nose and its position, the shape of the mouth, what kind of teeth and for what are they fitted? The shape and use of the tongue, are there any whiskers or feelers about the mouth?

4. Are the legs long or short? How many toes on the front feet and hind feet? Are they armed with claws? Are the feet padded? Are the legs and feet fitted for running, leaping, creeping, grasping, or clinging? Is the tail long or short? What is its covering? What is its use? How is the animal covered? How does its covering protect it? What is its color above and below? Does it help the animal to hide from its enemies or is it ornamental?

5. On what does the animal feed? How does it gets its food? If it carries its food, how?

6. Does it live on or beneath the ground or in trees, or in water or elsewhere?

7. Does it live alone or with mate or in a herd or flock?

8. Is it active during the day or night?

9. Where is its home, how is it made and how is it kept? Is it for itself or for its young?

10. Are its movements quick and active, strong and bold, stealthy or shy? Does it walk, run, leap or dart?

11. Where and in what position does it sleep?

12. How does it play? How does it show anger, pleasure, fear?

13. Has it a voice, if so, describe its uses.

14. How does it keep clean?

15. How does it care for its young? Do both parents take part in this? How are the young fed, carried, kept clean, defended, protected and taught to care for themselves? Are the young ever punished, if so, how?

16. How does this animal escape from its enemies? How does it fight them?

17. How does it live through winter?

The Elephant

THE STORY OF THE ELEPHANT

Date ....

Name of Animal ....

1. Is it domesticated or wild?

2. Estimate it's length and height.

3. Study the head: the shape of the ears, how placed, are they movable? The color, size and position of the eyes, the form of the nose and its position, the shape of the mouth, what kind of teeth and for what are they fitted? The shape and use of the tongue, are there any whiskers or feelers about the mouth?

4. Are the legs long or short? How many toes on the front feet and hind feet? Are they armed with claws? Are the feet padded? Are the legs and feet fitted for running, leaping, creeping, grasping, or clinging? Is the tail long or short? What is its covering? What is its use? How is the animal covered? How does its covering protect it? What is its color above and below? Does it help the animal to hide from its enemies or is it ornamental?

5. On what does the animal feed? How does it gets its food? If it carries its food, how?

6. Does it live on or beneath the ground or in trees, or in water or elsewhere?

7. Does it live alone or with mate or in a herd or flock?

8. Is it active during the day or night?

9. Where is its home, how is it made and how is it kept? Is it for itself or for its young?

10. Are its movements quick and active, strong and bold, stealthy or shy? Does it walk, run, leap or dart?

11. Where and in what position does it sleep?

12. How does it play? How does it show anger, pleasure, fear?

13. Has it a voice, if so, describe its uses.

14. How does it keep clean?

15. How does it care for its young? Do both parents take part in this? How are the young fed, carried, kept clean, defended, protected and taught to care for themselves? Are the young ever punished, if so, how?

16. How does this animal escape from its enemies? How does it fight them?

17. How does it live through winter?

NOTES ON THE GIRAFFE

The Giraffe

THE STORY OF THE GIRAFFE

OUTLINE FOR STUDY OF AN ANIMAL

Date ....

Name of Animal ....

1. Is it domesticated or wild?

2. Estimate it's length and height.

3. Study the head: the shape of the ears, how placed, are they movable? The color, size and position of the eyes, the form of the nose and its position, the shape of the mouth, what kind of teeth and for what are they fitted? The shape and use of the tongue, are there any whiskers or feelers about the mouth?

4. Are the legs long or short? How many toes on the front feet and hind feet? Are they armed with claws? Are the feet padded? Are the legs and feet fitted for running, leaping, creeping, grasping, or clinging? Is the tail long or short? What is its covering? What is its use? How is the animal covered? How does its covering protect it? What is its color above and below? Does it help the animal to hide from its enemies or is it ornamental?

5. On what does the animal feed? How does it gets its food? If it carries its food, how?

6. Does it live on or beneath the ground or in trees, or in water or elsewhere?

7. Does it live alone or with mate or in a herd or flock?

8. Is it active during the day or night?

9. Where is its home, how is it made and how is it kept? Is it for itself or for its young?

10. Are its movements quick and active, strong and bold, stealthy or shy? Does it walk, run, leap or dart?

11. Where and in what position does it sleep?

12. How does it play? How does it show anger, pleasure, fear?

13. Has it a voice, if so, describe its uses.

14. How does it keep clean?

15. How does it care for its young? Do both parents take part in this? How are the young fed, carried, kept clean, defended, protected and taught to care for themselves? Are the young ever punished, if so, how?

16. How does this animal escape from its enemies? How does it fight them?

17. How does it live through winter?

NOTES ON THE GORILLA

The Gorilla

Date ....

Name of Animal ....

1. Is it domesticated or wild?

2. Estimate it's length and height.

3. Study the head: the shape of the ears, how placed, are they movable? The color, size and position of the eyes, the form of the nose and its position, the shape of the mouth, what kind of teeth and for what are they fitted? The shape and use of the tongue, are there any whiskers or feelers about the mouth?

4. Are the legs long or short? How many toes on the front feet and hind feet? Are they armed with claws? Are the feet padded? Are the legs and feet fitted for running, leaping, creeping, grasping, or clinging? Is the tail long or short? What is its covering? What is its use? How is the animal covered? How does its covering protect it? What is its color above and below? Does it help the animal to hide from its enemies or is it ornamental?

5. On what does the animal feed? How does it gets its food? If it carries its food, how?

6. Does it live on or beneath the ground or in trees, or in water or elsewhere?

7. Does it live alone or with mate or in a herd or flock?

8. Is it active during the day or night?

9. Where is its home, how is it made and how is it kept? Is it for itself or for its young?

10. Are its movements quick and active, strong and bold, stealthy or shy? Does it walk, run, leap or dart?

11. Where and in what position does it sleep?

12. How does it play? How does it show anger, pleasure, fear?

13. Has it a voice, if so, describe its uses.

14. How does it keep clean?

15. How does it care for its young? Do both parents take part in this? How are the young fed, carried, kept clean, defended, protected and taught to care for themselves? Are the young ever punished, if so, how?

16. How does this animal escape from its enemies? How does it fight them?

17. How does it live through winter?

NOTES ON THE GRAY FOX

49

The Gray Fox

THE STORY OF THE GRAY FOX

Date ....

Name of Animal ....

1. Is it domesticated or wild?

2. Estimate it's length and height.

3. Study the head: the shape of the ears, how placed, are they movable? The color, size and position of the eyes, the form of the nose and its position, the shape of the mouth, what kind of teeth and for what are they fitted? The shape and use of the tongue, are there any whiskers or feelers about the mouth?

4. Are the legs long or short? How many toes on the front feet and hind feet? Are they armed with claws? Are the feet padded? Are the legs and feet fitted for running, leaping, creeping, grasping, or clinging? Is the tail long or short? What is its covering? What is its use? How is the animal covered? How does its covering protect it? What is its color above and below? Does it help the animal to hide from its enemies or is it ornamental?

5. On what does the animal feed? How does it gets its food? If it carries its food, how?

6. Does it live on or beneath the ground or in trees, or in water or elsewhere?

7. Does it live alone or with mate or in a herd or flock?

8. Is it active during the day or night?

9. Where is its home, how is it made and how is it kept? Is it for itself or for its young?

10. Are its movements quick and active, strong and bold, stealthy or shy? Does it walk, run, leap or dart?

11. Where and in what position does it sleep?

12. How does it play? How does it show anger, pleasure, fear?

13. Has it a voice, if so, describe its uses.

14. How does it keep clean?

15. How does it care for its young? Do both parents take part in this? How are the young fed, carried, kept clean, defended, protected and taught to care for themselves? Are the young ever punished, if so, how?

16. How does this animal escape from its enemies? How does it fight them?

17. How does it live through winter?

OUTLINE FOR STUDY OF AN ANIMAL

Date ....

Name of Animal ....

1. Is it domesticated or wild?

2. Estimate it's length and height.

3. Study the head: the shape of the ears, how placed, are they movable? The color, size and position of the eyes, the form of the nose and its position, the shape of the mouth, what kind of teeth and for what are they fitted? The shape and use of the tongue, are there any whiskers or feelers about the mouth?

4. Are the legs long or short? How many toes on the front feet and hind feet? Are they armed with claws? Are the feet padded? Are the legs and feet fitted for running, leaping, creeping, grasping, or clinging? Is the tail long or short? What is its covering? What is its use? How is the animal covered? How does its covering protect it? What is its color above and below? Does it help the animal to hide from its enemies or is it ornamental?

5. On what does the animal feed? How does it gets its food? If it carries its food, how?

6. Does it live on or beneath the ground or in trees, or in water or elsewhere?

7. Does it live alone or with mate or in a herd or flock?

8. Is it active during the day or night?

9. Where is its home, how is it made and how is it kept? Is it for itself or for its young?

10. Are its movements quick and active, strong and bold, stealthy or shy? Does it walk, run, leap or dart?

11. Where and in what position does it sleep?

12. How does it play? How does it show anger, pleasure, fear?

13. Has it a voice, if so, describe its uses.

14. How does it keep clean?

15. How does it care for its young? Do both parents take part in this? How are the young fed, carried, kept clean, defended, protected and taught to care for themselves? Are the young ever punished, if so, how?

16. How does this animal escape from its enemies? How does it fight them?

17. How does it live through winter?

NOTES ON THE HIPPOPOTAMUS

The Hippopotamus

THE STORY OF THE HIPPOPOTAMUS

Date ....

Name of Animal ....

1. Is it domesticated or wild?

2. Estimate it's length and height.

3. Study the head: the shape of the ears, how placed, are they movable? The color, size and position of the eyes, the form of the nose and its position, the shape of the mouth, what kind of teeth and for what are they fitted? The shape and use of the tongue, are there any whiskers or feelers about the mouth?

4. Are the legs long or short? How many toes on the front feet and hind feet? Are they armed with claws? Are the feet padded? Are the legs and feet fitted for running, leaping, creeping, grasping, or clinging? Is the tail long or short? What is its covering? What is its use? How is the animal covered? How does its covering protect it? What is its color above and below? Does it help the animal to hide from its enemies or is it ornamental?

5. On what does the animal feed? How does it gets its food? If it carries its food, how?

6. Does it live on or beneath the ground or in trees, or in water or elsewhere?

7. Does it live alone or with mate or in a herd or flock?

8. Is it active during the day or night?

9. Where is its home, how is it made and how is it kept? Is it for itself or for its young?

10. Are its movements quick and active, strong and bold, stealthy or shy? Does it walk, run, leap or dart?

11. Where and in what position does it sleep?

12. How does it play? How does it show anger, pleasure, fear?

13. Has it a voice, if so, describe its uses.

14. How does it keep clean?

15. How does it care for its young? Do both parents take part in this? How are the young fed, carried, kept clean, defended, protected and taught to care for themselves? Are the young ever punished, if so, how?

16. How does this animal escape from its enemies? How does it fight them?

17. How does it live through winter?

NOTES ON THE IBEX

The Ibex

THE STORY OF THE IBEX

Date ....

Name of Animal ....

1. Is it domesticated or wild?

2. Estimate it's length and height.

3. Study the head: the shape of the ears, how placed, are they movable? The color, size and position of the eyes, the form of the nose and its position, the shape of the mouth, what kind of teeth and for what are they fitted? The shape and use of the tongue, are there any whiskers or feelers about the mouth?

4. Are the legs long or short? How many toes on the front feet and hind feet? Are they armed with claws? Are the feet padded? Are the legs and feet fitted for running, leaping, creeping, grasping, or clinging? Is the tail long or short? What is its covering? What is its use? How is the animal covered? How does its covering protect it? What is its color above and below? Does it help the animal to hide from its enemies or is it ornamental?

5. On what does the animal feed? How does it gets its food? If it carries its food, how?

6. Does it live on or beneath the ground or in trees, or in water or elsewhere?

7. Does it live alone or with mate or in a herd or flock?

8. Is it active during the day or night?

9. Where is its home, how is it made and how is it kept? Is it for itself or for its young?

10. Are its movements quick and active, strong and bold, stealthy or shy? Does it walk, run, leap or dart?

11. Where and in what position does it sleep?

12. How does it play? How does it show anger, pleasure, fear?

13. Has it a voice, if so, describe its uses.

14. How does it keep clean?

15. How does it care for its young? Do both parents take part in this? How are the young fed, carried, kept clean, defended, protected and taught to care for themselves? Are the young ever punished, if so, how?

16. How does this animal escape from its enemies? How does it fight them?

17. How does it live through winter?

NOTES ON THE JAGUAR

The Jaguar

THE STORY OF THE JAGUAR

Date ....

Name of Animal ....

1. Is it domesticated or wild?

2. Estimate it's length and height.

3. Study the head: the shape of the ears, how placed, are they movable? The color, size and position of the eyes, the form of the nose and its position, the shape of the mouth, what kind of teeth and for what are they fitted? The shape and use of the tongue, are there any whiskers or feelers about the mouth?

4. Are the legs long or short? How many toes on the front feet and hind feet? Are they armed with claws? Are the feet padded? Are the legs and feet fitted for running, leaping, creeping, grasping, or clinging? Is the tail long or short? What is its covering? What is its use? How is the animal covered? How does its covering protect it? What is its color above and below? Does it help the animal to hide from its enemies or is it ornamental?

5. On what does the animal feed? How does it gets its food? If it carries its food, how?

6. Does it live on or beneath the ground or in trees, or in water or elsewhere?

7. Does it live alone or with mate or in a herd or flock?

8. Is it active during the day or night?

9. Where is its home, how is it made and how is it kept? Is it for itself or for its young?

10. Are its movements quick and active, strong and bold, stealthy or shy? Does it walk, run, leap or dart?

11. Where and in what position does it sleep?

12. How does it play? How does it show anger, pleasure, fear?

13. Has it a voice, if so, describe its uses.

14. How does it keep clean?

15. How does it care for its young? Do both parents take part in this? How are the young fed, carried, kept clean, defended, protected and taught to care for themselves? Are the young ever punished, if so, how?

16. How does this animal escape from its enemies? How does it fight them?

17. How does it live through winter?

NOTES ON THE KANGAROO

The Kangaroo

THE STORY OF THE KANGAROO

Outline for Study of an Animal

Date ....

Name of Animal ....

1. Is it domesticated or wild?

2. Estimate it's length and height.

3. Study the head: the shape of the ears, how placed, are they movable? The color, size and position of the eyes, the form of the nose and its position, the shape of the mouth, what kind of teeth and for what are they fitted? The shape and use of the tongue, are there any whiskers or feelers about the mouth?

4. Are the legs long or short? How many toes on the front feet and hind feet? Are they armed with claws? Are the feet padded? Are the legs and feet fitted for running, leaping, creeping, grasping, or clinging? Is the tail long or short? What is its covering? What is its use? How is the animal covered? How does its covering protect it? What is its color above and below? Does it help the animal to hide from its enemies or is it ornamental?

5. On what does the animal feed? How does it gets its food? If it carries its food, how?

6. Does it live on or beneath the ground or in trees, or in water or elsewhere?

7. Does it live alone or with mate or in a herd or flock?

8. Is it active during the day or night?

9. Where is its home, how is it made and how is it kept? Is it for itself or for its young?

10. Are its movements quick and active, strong and bold, stealthy or shy? Does it walk, run, leap or dart?

11. Where and in what position does it sleep?

12. How does it play? How does it show anger, pleasure, fear?

13. Has it a voice, if so, describe its uses.

14. How does it keep clean?

15. How does it care for its young? Do both parents take part in this? How are the young fed, carried, kept clean, defended, protected and taught to care for themselves? Are the young ever punished, if so, how?

16. How does this animal escape from its enemies? How does it fight them?

17. How does it live through winter?

The Leopard

THE STORY OF THE LEOPARD

OUTLINE FOR STUDY OF AN ANIMAL

Date ....

Name of Animal ....

1. Is it domesticated or wild?

2. Estimate it's length and height.

3. Study the head: the shape of the ears, how placed, are they movable? The color, size and position of the eyes, the form of the nose and its position, the shape of the mouth, what kind of teeth and for what are they fitted? The shape and use of the tongue, are there any whiskers or feelers about the mouth?

4. Are the legs long or short? How many toes on the front feet and hind feet? Are they armed with claws? Are the feet padded? Are the legs and feet fitted for running, leaping, creeping, grasping, or clinging? Is the tail long or short? What is its covering? What is its use? How is the animal covered? How does its covering protect it? What is its color above and below? Does it help the animal to hide from its enemies or is it ornamental?

5. On what does the animal feed? How does it gets its food? If it carries its food, how?

6. Does it live on or beneath the ground or in trees, or in water or elsewhere?

7. Does it live alone or with mate or in a herd or flock?

8. Is it active during the day or night?

9. Where is its home, how is it made and how is it kept? Is it for itself or for its young?

10. Are its movements quick and active, strong and bold, stealthy or shy? Does it walk, run, leap or dart?

11. Where and in what position does it sleep?

12. How does it play? How does it show anger, pleasure, fear?

13. Has it a voice, if so, describe its uses.

14. How does it keep clean?

15. How does it care for its young? Do both parents take part in this? How are the young fed, carried, kept clean, defended, protected and taught to care for themselves? Are the young ever punished, if so, how?

16. How does this animal escape from its enemies? How does it fight them?

17. How does it live through winter?

NOTES ON THE LION

The Lion

THE STORY OF THE LION

Date ....

Name of Animal ....

1. Is it domesticated or wild?

2. Estimate it's length and height.

3. Study the head: the shape of the ears, how placed, are they movable? The color, size and position of the eyes, the form of the nose and its position, the shape of the mouth, what kind of teeth and for what are they fitted? The shape and use of the tongue, are there any whiskers or feelers about the mouth?

4. Are the legs long or short? How many toes on the front feet and hind feet? Are they armed with claws? Are the feet padded? Are the legs and feet fitted for running, leaping, creeping, grasping, or clinging? Is the tail long or short? What is its covering? What is its use? How is the animal covered? How does its covering protect it? What is its color above and below? Does it help the animal to hide from its enemies or is it ornamental?

5. On what does the animal feed? How does it gets its food? If it carries its food, how?

6. Does it live on or beneath the ground or in trees, or in water or elsewhere?

7. Does it live alone or with mate or in a herd or flock?

8. Is it active during the day or night?

9. Where is its home, how is it made and how is it kept? Is it for itself or for its young?

10. Are its movements quick and active, strong and bold, stealthy or shy? Does it walk, run, leap or dart?

11. Where and in what position does it sleep?

12. How does it play? How does it show anger, pleasure, fear?

13. Has it a voice, if so, describe its uses.

14. How does it keep clean?

15. How does it care for its young? Do both parents take part in this? How are the young fed, carried, kept clean, defended, protected and taught to care for themselves? Are the young ever punished, if so, how?

16. How does this animal escape from its enemies? How does it fight them?

17. How does it live through winter?

The Llama

THE STORY OF THE LLAMA

Date ....

Name of Animal ....

1. Is it domesticated or wild?

2. Estimate it's length and height.

3. Study the head: the shape of the ears, how placed, are they movable? The color, size and position of the eyes, the form of the nose and its position, the shape of the mouth, what kind of teeth and for what are they fitted? The shape and use of the tongue, are there any whiskers or feelers about the mouth?

4. Are the legs long or short? How many toes on the front feet and hind feet? Are they armed with claws? Are the feet padded? Are the legs and feet fitted for running, leaping, creeping, grasping, or clinging? Is the tail long or short? What is its covering? What is its use? How is the animal covered? How does its covering protect it? What is its color above and below? Does it help the animal to hide from its enemies or is it ornamental?

5. On what does the animal feed? How does it gets its food? If it carries its food, how?

6. Does it live on or beneath the ground or in trees, or in water or elsewhere?

7. Does it live alone or with mate or in a herd or flock?

8. Is it active during the day or night?

9. Where is its home, how is it made and how is it kept? Is it for itself or for its young?

10. Are its movements quick and active, strong and bold, stealthy or shy? Does it walk, run, leap or dart?

11. Where and in what position does it sleep?

12. How does it play? How does it show anger, pleasure, fear?

13. Has it a voice, if so, describe its uses.

14. How does it keep clean?

15. How does it care for its young? Do both parents take part in this? How are the young fed, carried, kept clean, defended, protected and taught to care for themselves? Are the young ever punished, if so, how?

16. How does this animal escape from its enemies? How does it fight them?

17. How does it live through winter?

NOTES ON THE LYNX

The Lynx

THE STORY OF THE LYNX

Outline for Study of an Animal

Date ....

Name of Animal ....

1. Is it domesticated or wild?

2. Estimate it's length and height.

3. Study the head: the shape of the ears, how placed, are they movable? The color, size and position of the eyes, the form of the nose and its position, the shape of the mouth, what kind of teeth and for what are they fitted? The shape and use of the tongue, are there any whiskers or feelers about the mouth?

4. Are the legs long or short? How many toes on the front feet and hind feet? Are they armed with claws? Are the feet padded? Are the legs and feet fitted for running, leaping, creeping, grasping, or clinging? Is the tail long or short? What is its covering? What is its use? How is the animal covered? How does its covering protect it? What is its color above and below? Does it help the animal to hide from its enemies or is it ornamental?

5. On what does the animal feed? How does it gets its food? If it carries its food, how?

6. Does it live on or beneath the ground or in trees, or in water or elsewhere?

7. Does it live alone or with mate or in a herd or flock?

8. Is it active during the day or night?

9. Where is its home, how is it made and how is it kept? Is it for itself or for its young?

10. Are its movements quick and active, strong and bold, stealthy or shy? Does it walk, run, leap or dart?

11. Where and in what position does it sleep?

12. How does it play? How does it show anger, pleasure, fear?

13. Has it a voice, if so, describe its uses.

14. How does it keep clean?

15. How does it care for its young? Do both parents take part in this? How are the young fed, carried, kept clean, defended, protected and taught to care for themselves? Are the young ever punished, if so, how?

16. How does this animal escape from its enemies? How does it fight them?

17. How does it live through winter?

88

NOTES ON THE MONKEYS

Monkeys

Capuchin and Rhesus

OUTLINE FOR STUDY OF AN ANIMAL

Date ....

Name of Animal ....

1. Is it domesticated or wild?

2. Estimate it's length and height.

3. Study the head: the shape of the ears, how placed, are they movable? The color, size and position of the eyes, the form of the nose and its position, the shape of the mouth, what kind of teeth and for what are they fitted? The shape and use of the tongue, are there any whiskers or feelers about the mouth?

4. Are the legs long or short? How many toes on the front feet and hind feet? Are they armed with claws? Are the feet padded? Are the legs and feet fitted for running, leaping, creeping, grasping, or clinging? Is the tail long or short? What is its covering? What is its use? How is the animal covered? How does its covering protect it? What is its color above and below? Does it help the animal to hide from its enemies or is it ornamental?

5. On what does the animal feed? How does it gets its food? If it carries its food, how?

6. Does it live on or beneath the ground or in trees, or in water or elsewhere?

7. Does it live alone or with mate or in a herd or flock?

8. Is it active during the day or night?

9. Where is its home, how is it made and how is it kept? Is it for itself or for its young?

10. Are its movements quick and active, strong and bold, stealthy or shy? Does it walk, run, leap or dart?

11. Where and in what position does it sleep?

12. How does it play? How does it show anger, pleasure, fear?

13. Has it a voice, if so, describe its uses.

14. How does it keep clean?

15. How does it care for its young? Do both parents take part in this? How are the young fed, carried, kept clean, defended, protected and taught to care for themselves? Are the young ever punished, if so, how?

16. How does this animal escape from its enemies? How does it fight them?

17. How does it live through winter?

92

NOTES ON THE OTTER

The Otter

THE STORY OF THE OTTER

Date ....

Name of Animal ....

1. Is it domesticated or wild?

2. Estimate it's length and height.

3. Study the head: the shape of the ears, how placed, are they movable? The color, size and position of the eyes, the form of the nose and its position, the shape of the mouth, what kind of teeth and for what are they fitted? The shape and use of the tongue, are there any whiskers or feelers about the mouth?

4. Are the legs long or short? How many toes on the front feet and hind feet? Are they armed with claws? Are the feet padded? Are the legs and feet fitted for running, leaping, creeping, grasping, or clinging? Is the tail long or short? What is its covering? What is its use? How is the animal covered? How does its covering protect it? What is its color above and below? Does it help the animal to hide from its enemies or is it ornamental?

5. On what does the animal feed? How does it gets its food? If it carries its food, how?

6. Does it live on or beneath the ground or in trees, or in water or elsewhere?

7. Does it live alone or with mate or in a herd or flock?

8. Is it active during the day or night?

9. Where is its home, how is it made and how is it kept? Is it for itself or for its young?

10. Are its movements quick and active, strong and bold, stealthy or shy? Does it walk, run, leap or dart?

11. Where and in what position does it sleep?

12. How does it play? How does it show anger, pleasure, fear?

13. Has it a voice, if so, describe its uses.

14. How does it keep clean?

15. How does it care for its young? Do both parents take part in this? How are the young fed, carried, kept clean, defended, protected and taught to care for themselves? Are the young ever punished, if so, how?

16. How does this animal escape from its enemies? How does it fight them?

17. How does it live through winter?

The Polar Bear

THE STORY OF THE POLAR BEAR

OUTLINE FOR STUDY OF AN ANIMAL

Date ....

Name of Animal ....

1. Is it domesticated or wild?

2. Estimate it's length and height.

3. Study the head: the shape of the ears, how placed, are they movable? The color, size and position of the eyes, the form of the nose and its position, the shape of the mouth, what kind of teeth and for what are they fitted? The shape and use of the tongue, are there any whiskers or feelers about the mouth?

4. Are the legs long or short? How many toes on the front feet and hind feet? Are they armed with claws? Are the feet padded? Are the legs and feet fitted for running, leaping, creeping, grasping, or clinging? Is the tail long or short? What is its covering? What is its use? How is the animal covered? How does its covering protect it? What is its color above and below? Does it help the animal to hide from its enemies or is it ornamental?

5. On what does the animal feed? How does it gets its food? If it carries its food, how?

6. Does it live on or beneath the ground or in trees, or in water or elsewhere?

7. Does it live alone or with mate or in a herd or flock?

8. Is it active during the day or night?

9. Where is its home, how is it made and how is it kept? Is it for itself or for its young?

10. Are its movements quick and active, strong and bold, stealthy or shy? Does it walk, run, leap or dart?

11. Where and in what position does it sleep?

12. How does it play? How does it show anger, pleasure, fear?

13. Has it a voice, if so, describe its uses.

14. How does it keep clean?

15. How does it care for its young? Do both parents take part in this? How are the young fed, carried, kept clean, defended, protected and taught to care for themselves? Are the young ever punished, if so, how?

16. How does this animal escape from its enemies? How does it fight them?

17. How does it live through winter?

100

NOTES ON THE RED FOX

The Red Fox

THE STORY OF THE RED FOX

Date ....

Name of Animal ....

1. Is it domesticated or wild?

2. Estimate it's length and height.

3. Study the head: the shape of the ears, how placed, are they movable? The color, size and position of the eyes, the form of the nose and its position, the shape of the mouth, what kind of teeth and for what are they fitted? The shape and use of the tongue, are there any whiskers or feelers about the mouth?

4. Are the legs long or short? How many toes on the front feet and hind feet? Are they armed with claws? Are the feet padded? Are the legs and feet fitted for running, leaping, creeping, grasping, or clinging? Is the tail long or short? What is its covering? What is its use? How is the animal covered? How does its covering protect it? What is its color above and below? Does it help the animal to hide from its enemies or is it ornamental?

5. On what does the animal feed? How does it gets its food? If it carries its food, how?

6. Does it live on or beneath the ground or in trees, or in water or elsewhere?

7. Does it live alone or with mate or in a herd or flock?

8. Is it active during the day or night?

9. Where is its home, how is it made and how is it kept? Is it for itself or for its young?

10. Are its movements quick and active, strong and bold, stealthy or shy? Does it walk, run, leap or dart?

11. Where and in what position does it sleep?

12. How does it play? How does it show anger, pleasure, fear?

13. Has it a voice, if so, describe its uses.

14. How does it keep clean?

15. How does it care for its young? Do both parents take part in this? How are the young fed, carried, kept clean, defended, protected and taught to care for themselves? Are the young ever punished, if so, how?

16. How does this animal escape from its enemies? How does it fight them?

17. How does it live through winter?

NOTES ON THE RHINOCEROS

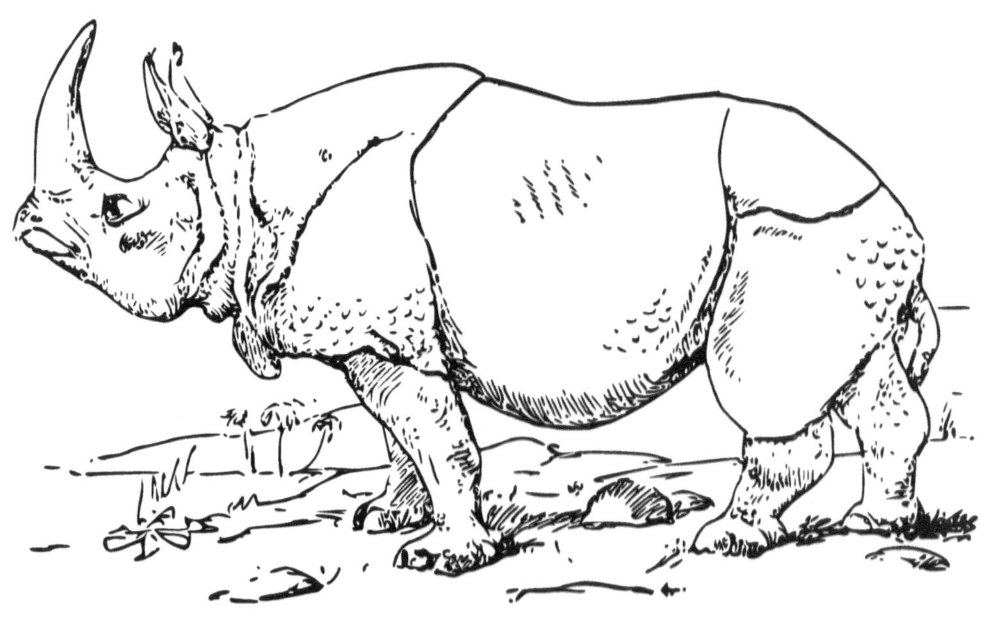

THE STORY OF THE RHINOCEROS

Date ....

Name of Animal ....

1. Is it domesticated or wild?

2. Estimate it's length and height.

3. Study the head: the shape of the ears, how placed, are they movable? The color, size and position of the eyes, the form of the nose and its position, the shape of the mouth, what kind of teeth and for what are they fitted? The shape and use of the tongue, are there any whiskers or feelers about the mouth?

4. Are the legs long or short? How many toes on the front feet and hind feet? Are they armed with claws? Are the feet padded? Are the legs and feet fitted for running, leaping, creeping, grasping, or clinging? Is the tail long or short? What is its covering? What is its use? How is the animal covered? How does its covering protect it? What is its color above and below? Does it help the animal to hide from its enemies or is it ornamental?

5. On what does the animal feed? How does it gets its food? If it carries its food, how?

6. Does it live on or beneath the ground or in trees, or in water or elsewhere?

7. Does it live alone or with mate or in a herd or flock?

8. Is it active during the day or night?

9. Where is its home, how is it made and how is it kept? Is it for itself or for its young?

10. Are its movements quick and active, strong and bold, stealthy or shy? Does it walk, run, leap or dart?

11. Where and in what position does it sleep?

12. How does it play? How does it show anger, pleasure, fear?

13. Has it a voice, if so, describe its uses.

14. How does it keep clean?

15. How does it care for its young? Do both parents take part in this? How are the young fed, carried, kept clean, defended, protected and taught to care for themselves? Are the young ever punished, if so, how?

16. How does this animal escape from its enemies? How does it fight them?

17. How does it live through winter?

NOTES ON THE TAPIR

The Tapir

THE STORY OF THE TAPIR

Date ....

Name of Animal ....

1. Is it domesticated or wild?

2. Estimate it's length and height.

3. Study the head: the shape of the ears, how placed, are they movable? The color, size and position of the eyes, the form of the nose and its position, the shape of the mouth, what kind of teeth and for what are they fitted? The shape and use of the tongue, are there any whiskers or feelers about the mouth?

4. Are the legs long or short? How many toes on the front feet and hind feet? Are they armed with claws? Are the feet padded? Are the legs and feet fitted for running, leaping, creeping, grasping, or clinging? Is the tail long or short? What is its covering? What is its use? How is the animal covered? How does its covering protect it? What is its color above and below? Does it help the animal to hide from its enemies or is it ornamental?

5. On what does the animal feed? How does it gets its food? If it carries its food, how?

6. Does it live on or beneath the ground or in trees, or in water or elsewhere?

7. Does it live alone or with mate or in a herd or flock?

8. Is it active during the day or night?

9. Where is its home, how is it made and how is it kept? Is it for itself or for its young?

10. Are its movements quick and active, strong and bold, stealthy or shy? Does it walk, run, leap or dart?

11. Where and in what position does it sleep?

12. How does it play? How does it show anger, pleasure, fear?

13. Has it a voice, if so, describe its uses.

14. How does it keep clean?

15. How does it care for its young? Do both parents take part in this? How are the young fed, carried, kept clean, defended, protected and taught to care for themselves? Are the young ever punished, if so, how?

16. How does this animal escape from its enemies? How does it fight them?

17. How does it live through winter?

NOTES ON THE TIGER

The Tiger

Date ....

Name of Animal ....

1. Is it domesticated or wild?

2. Estimate it's length and height.

3. Study the head: the shape of the ears, how placed, are they movable? The color, size and position of the eyes, the form of the nose and its position, the shape of the mouth, what kind of teeth and for what are they fitted? The shape and use of the tongue, are there any whiskers or feelers about the mouth?

4. Are the legs long or short? How many toes on the front feet and hind feet? Are they armed with claws? Are the feet padded? Are the legs and feet fitted for running, leaping, creeping, grasping, or clinging? Is the tail long or short? What is its covering? What is its use? How is the animal covered? How does its covering protect it? What is its color above and below? Does it help the animal to hide from its enemies or is it ornamental?

5. On what does the animal feed? How does it gets its food? If it carries its food, how?

6. Does it live on or beneath the ground or in trees, or in water or elsewhere?

7. Does it live alone or with mate or in a herd or flock?

8. Is it active during the day or night?

9. Where is its home, how is it made and how is it kept? Is it for itself or for its young?

10. Are its movements quick and active, strong and bold, stealthy or shy? Does it walk, run, leap or dart?

11. Where and in what position does it sleep?

12. How does it play? How does it show anger, pleasure, fear?

13. Has it a voice, if so, describe its uses.

14. How does it keep clean?

15. How does it care for its young? Do both parents take part in this? How are the young fed, carried, kept clean, defended, protected and taught to care for themselves? Are the young ever punished, if so, how?

16. How does this animal escape from its enemies? How does it fight them?

17. How does it live through winter?

NOTES ON THE WOLF

The Wolf

Date ....

Name of Animal ....

1. Is it domesticated or wild?

2. Estimate it's length and height.

3. Study the head: the shape of the ears, how placed, are they movable? The color, size and position of the eyes, the form of the nose and its position, the shape of the mouth, what kind of teeth and for what are they fitted? The shape and use of the tongue, are there any whiskers or feelers about the mouth?

4. Are the legs long or short? How many toes on the front feet and hind feet? Are they armed with claws? Are the feet padded? Are the legs and feet fitted for running, leaping, creeping, grasping, or clinging? Is the tail long or short? What is its covering? What is its use? How is the animal covered? How does its covering protect it? What is its color above and below? Does it help the animal to hide from its enemies or is it ornamental?

5. On what does the animal feed? How does it gets its food? If it carries its food, how?

6. Does it live on or beneath the ground or in trees, or in water or elsewhere?

7. Does it live alone or with mate or in a herd or flock?

8. Is it active during the day or night?

9. Where is its home, how is it made and how is it kept? Is it for itself or for its young?

10. Are its movements quick and active, strong and bold, stealthy or shy? Does it walk, run, leap or dart?

11. Where and in what position does it sleep?

12. How does it play? How does it show anger, pleasure, fear?

13. Has it a voice, if so, describe its uses.

14. How does it keep clean?

15. How does it care for its young? Do both parents take part in this? How are the young fed, carried, kept clean, defended, protected and taught to care for themselves? Are the young ever punished, if so, how?

16. How does this animal escape from its enemies? How does it fight them?

17. How does it live through winter?

The Zebra

THE STORY OF THE ZEBRA